"You want me t[...]
mentor. Not g[...]

Megan's mouth dropped open. "What!"

Harry arched an eyebrow. "Did I stutter? It's not going to happen. You shouldn't have messed with me when you first came to work here."

She gestured wildly. "Are you insane? We can't stand each other! You've done nothing but pick apart my performance since I got here. Let me have a different mentor."

Megan drew a deep breath as if trying to calm herself. Her suit jacket gaped open. She was wearing white lace. Harry's throat went dry, and his words simply disappeared.

"No."

THE PLAYBOY'S PROTÉGÉE

Michele Dunaway

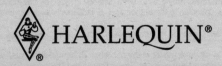

HARLEQUIN®

TORONTO • NEW YORK • LONDON
AMSTERDAM • PARIS • SYDNEY • HAMBURG
STOCKHOLM • ATHENS • TOKYO • MILAN • MADRID
PRAGUE • WARSAW • BUDAPEST • AUCKLAND

For Uncle Bizz ('cos it already is)

ISBN 0-373-16988-4

THE PLAYBOY'S PROTÉGÉE

Copyright © 2003 by Michele Dunaway.

This edition published by arrangement with Harlequin Books S.A.

® and TM are trademarks of the publisher. Trademarks indicated with
® are registered in the United States Patent and Trademark Office, the
Canadian Trade Marks Office and in other countries.

Visit us at www.eHarlequin.com

Printed in U.S.A.

AUTHOR'S NOTE

In the story, Megan's mother suffers from multiple sclerosis (MS). My cousin Stacey lives daily with MS, and she was an invaluable source of information. Any errors in the story are mine. For more information about this disease, contact The National Multiple Sclerosis Society, 733 Third Avenue, New York, NY 10017. www.nmss.org.

ABOUT THE AUTHOR

In first grade Michele Dunaway knew she wanted to be a teacher when she grew up, and by second grade she wanted to be an author. By third grade she was determined to be both. Born and raised in a west county suburb of St. Louis, Michele recently moved to five acres in the rolling hills of Labadie. She's traveled extensively, with the cities and places she visits often becoming settings for her stories.

Michele currently teaches high school English, raises her two young daughters and describes herself as a woman who does too much but doesn't want to stop.

Michele loves to hear from readers. You can visit her Web site at www.micheledunaway.com or write to her at P.O. Box 45, Labadie, MO 63055.

Books by Michele Dunaway

HARLEQUIN AMERICAN ROMANCE

★ ★ ★ ★ ★ ★ ★ ★ ★ ★ ★ ★ ★ ★ ★ ★ ★ ★

Jacobsen Stars Program:
Corporate Strategy for Future Marital Team
as Created by Grandpa Joe

The Key Players:

Megan MacGregor: Ambitious businesswoman, excellent mind, easy on the eyes. Perfect for Harry.

Harry Sanders: My ornery grandson who needs a swift kick (but most of all, a good wife).

Strategy:

Make them work together as a team, thereby encouraging opportunities for covert mingling, which will lead to marriage and happiness.

Obstacle to Strategy:

Megan and Harry hate each other.

Way around Obstacle:

Lock them in a hotel suite together, with all the usual amenities, i.e., champagne, strawberries, chocolate and terry-cloth bathrobes.

Motto:

Grandpa Joe will pave the way for Harry and Megan's happy day!

★ ★ ★ ★ ★ ★ ★ ★ ★ ★ ★ ★ ★ ★ ★ ★ ★ ★

Prologue

Jacobsen Enterprises Internal Memo
From: Joe Jacobsen, CEO
To: Harry Sanders
CC: Andrew Sanders, president
Re: Jacobsen Stars Program

Harry,
I just wanted to give you a heads up on the newest Jacobsen Enterprises program to recruit and retain upper-level management.

With your sister now in New York for the past year, it is imperative for the overall growth and stability of the firm that we keep any management talent we develop. My proposal will be instituted in two weeks, and a copy is attached. I would like you to personally consider being a mentor. If you have any questions, don't hesitate to contact me.
J.J.

Jacobsen Enterprises Internal Memo
From: Joe Jacobsen, CEO
To: Andrew Sanders, president
Re: Harry/Jacobsen Stars

As you can see from my previous memo, I have informed your son about the Jacobsen Stars program and have indicated that I would like him to be a mentor.

My personal choice for him to mentor is Megan MacGregor. I will drop in on him Monday morning to tell him. She's in Mergers and Acquisitions.
J.J.

Jacobsen Enterprises Internal Memo
From: Andrew Sanders, president
To: Joe Jacobsen, CEO
Re: Harry/Jacobsen Stars

You old coot. The only merger you really want is for your grandson to get married. But setting up Harry with Megan MacGregor? She'll eat him alive. Don't you ever stop matchmaking?
A.S.

Jacobsen Enterprises Internal Memo
From: Joe Jacobsen, CEO
To: Andrew Sanders, president
Re: Harry/Jacobsen Stars

No.
J.J.

Chapter One

Even though it was a Monday, it had all the makings of a wonderful day. As the only person in the executive elevator, Harry Sanders whistled the entire journey to his office on the twenty-second floor of the Jacobsen Enterprises world headquarters.

"You're chipper this morning," Peggy, his secretary for the past five years, commented as he strode over the plush carpet. Ten minutes before 9:00 a.m., she had already sorted his memos and mail.

"Absolutely," Harry said taking the stack of papers without stopping to look through them as he usually did.

He registered Peggy's words as he entered his office, "There's one from your grandfather."

There had better be. Harry smiled as he entered his corner office, and he took a minute to look out the window. Even though it was a beautiful May day, his office faced west and south, giving him a boring view of Highway 40 as it wound toward Jefferson Avenue.

The eastern-facing offices of the Jacobsen Building

looked down Market Street, the view encompassing Memorial Plaza, Union Station, the Mississippi riverfront, the Old Courthouse and the Gateway Arch.

No, his office view was not quite the best, or even on the top floor, that was the twenty-fifth floor, but all that was about to change.

And it was about time.

He pushed a strand of blond hair off his face. He'd been waiting for the past two years, and with Darci happily out of the way, it was finally Harry's time to shine.

He took a minute to think about that. Don't get him wrong, he loved his academically brilliant sister with the Harvard MBA. However, three years his junior, Darci had held a higher title and position in Jacobsen Enterprises before her resignation and subsequent move to New York City to be with Cameron O'Brien, her now-husband of one year.

Darci's fast rise through the company still rankled Harry, that and the fact that after she'd resigned, he hadn't been promoted into her spot. But given his grandfather's eccentricities and obvious favoritism toward his granddaughters, no one had been too surprised to see Darci's job left unfilled. The vice president of development position she'd held had just sort of faded away.

"Good, you're here early." Speaking of the devil. The voice that startled Harry from his reverie belonged to none other than Joe Jacobsen, and Harry turned to see his grandfather standing in the office doorway.

"I'm always on time," Harry replied. It was the truth. One thing Harry managed was timeliness.

Standing there looking like a thin version of Santa Claus, Grandpa Joe didn't even blink at Harry's answer. Even though the blue-eyed gene was recessive, every Jacobsen grandchild, including Harry, had the same blue eyes with a rim of dark blue that their grandfather had.

"Didn't say you were late. I know your schedule," Grandpa Joe said in the tone that meant no excuses, boy. "Did you read my memo yet?"

"No," Harry said.

So much for it looking to be a good day with a promotion on the horizon. A sense of foreboding filled Harry. He knew his eccentric if not business-brilliant grandfather too well. And although at six foot two Harry often towered over other men, the dynamic Grandpa Joe still made Harry occasionally feel like a small wayward child.

Harry began to sort through the papers Peggy had given him. As he found the memo, he said, "Here it is."

Grandpa Joe nodded, his thin white beard bobbing slightly. "Why don't you take a minute to read it."

As Harry scanned the memo he read the words aloud. "I just wanted to give you a heads up on the newest Jacobsen Enterprises program to recruit and retain upper-level management."

He looked up at Grandpa Joe, who was staring out the window. Harry's gaze flew over the rest of the memo outlining the new Jacobsen Stars program. A worried thought started in the pit of his stomach as he looked over at the spiral-bound presentation folder that was with the other mail on his desk. The sinking feeling quickly spread through the rest of his body.

"You want me to be a mentor?"

Grandpa Joe slowly turned around, his face a neutral mask. He gave a curt nod. "Absolutely."

Harry stared as his grandfather continued. "I quite like my idea, and given your position in the company, it will be a good way to expand your horizons and help out the Jacobsen team. I think it will be a good experience for you."

"A good experience for me?" Incredulity filled Harry's voice. "From the way you were talking two days ago, I thought you were going to fill the vice president of development position."

Grandpa Joe rolled his shoulders. "I'm still not sure about that yet."

At that moment, business relationship be darned. This was personal, this was family. Whatever his grandfather had up his sleeve a few days ago, it hadn't been this. "You're going to promote someone else over my head, aren't you? How is that a good experience for me?"

The neutral expression on his grandfather's face never changed. "No one said anything about promoting people. Stop putting words into my mouth. This program is all about keeping top talent in the company. We don't want them lured away by any of our competitors, especially after we've put so much investment into training them."

"What about me? Where do I fit into all this?"

Grandpa Joe blinked. "That's obvious, Harry, my boy, you're going to be a mentor. In fact, that's why I'm here. I've got the perfect person picked out just for you. She's a recent hire. Well, I guess a year ago isn't too recent. We hired her after Darci left. You know Megan MacGregor. She's in Mergers and Acquisitions. An absolute gem that girl is, and I want to make sure she stays with us. She has raw talent, and I think you can help develop it."

Megan MacGregor. Harry bit back the bile that immediately came to his throat upon hearing her name. He certainly did not want to mentor her. "I develop business opportunities and future growth," he said. "I do not develop talent in females."

"Your playboy reputation tells me that you at least try to develop something with females," Grandpa Joe said. There was hard steel underlining his voice. "And let me remind you that *Working Mother* named this company one of the best places to work in America. At Jacobsen Enterprises we take pride in knocking down the glass ceiling. But don't worry. You don't have to participate, Harry. After all, you are family, and you will always have a place in the company. I made that promise to your mother when you graduated high school and went off to Vanderbilt."

Wonderful, Harry thought. Grandpa Joe had wanted Harry, his oldest grandson, to go to Princeton. Accepted at both colleges, Harry had wanted to stay closer to Saint Louis. So he'd chosen Vanderbilt in Tennessee instead of the Ivy League Princeton in

New Jersey, much to Grandpa Joe's disappointment. Grandpa Joe had graduated from Princeton.

And by his grandfather bringing up Harry's choice of alma mater, Harry knew that once again he'd displeased Grandpa Joe.

Which probably meant that Harry was about to be passed over again for a better spot in the company. In reality, being family didn't even mean that much. Everyone knew that Grandpa Joe favored his grand-daughters over his grandsons. Look at poor Shane, the youngest of all the grandchildren. Grandpa Joe didn't even want him around, and hence Shane didn't work anywhere in the company. Instead, he lived in his parents' pool house and sponged off his trust fund. All the grandchildren had gotten a trust fund at age twenty-one, and Harry had tripled its value already.

Not that Grandpa Joe had ever mentioned that feat, a formidable accomplishment given the current stock-market crisis.

Heavy silence fell as Harry contemplated his options. How to get out of this situation gracefully? "I'd prefer that if I was going to mentor someone it be someone other than Megan MacGregor," Harry said finally. "Someone male preferably. I don't need to even get close to putting myself into a potential sexual harassment case."

"So you think Megan MacGregor is a sexual harassment case waiting to happen?" Uh-oh. That tone again.

Harry squared his chin. He knew Megan's type, but

he should have kept his mouth shut about his opinion of her kind. Too late now. "Yes. Yes, I do."

"Interesting," Grandpa Joe said. He tilted his head as if he was contemplating a new electronics purchase. "You may be right. I'll have to see what I can do. I have just about everyone else assigned, so it might take some juggling to move people around. If it won't work out, you just won't mentor. Let me get back to you." And with that said, Grandpa Joe left the office.

Harry blinked. Just like that, Grandpa Joe was really gone. Had Harry missed something? Where had the night-and-day change in his grandfather come from?

Or had there really been a change? Harry leaned forward. The leather chair thumped his back as he picked up the spiral-bound Jacobsen Stars binder. He thumbed through it, skimming the highlights of the program.

He tossed the binder down. The program was like handing Megan MacGregor the keys to the Jacobsen kingdom. Couldn't his grandfather see through her? She was a piranha both in business and her personal life. Although he hated listening to office gossip, according to the grapevine, she'd landed a man twenty years her senior for her fiancé. He'd been seen in her office.

Even the former floor receptionist, before she'd left, had blasted Megan MacGregor. No, Harry didn't want anything to do with her. She was the type that would stop at nothing to get what she wanted, even if it meant crawling over his dead body to do it.

The real claw was that Grandpa Joe obviously adored Megan. He'd discovered her, so to speak, and had personally overseen her Jacobsen career. Megan had replaced Darci. That meant Harry really needed to be on his toes. He couldn't let his guard down, especially when Megan MacGregor was involved.

FOR A MONDAY, it wasn't really that bad of a day. Megan MacGregor looked around, satisfied. Work that she'd thought would take two days had been miraculously finished in one. Not yet three in the afternoon, Megan discovered she could even see the bottom of her wood inbox.

She slid a report into an interoffice-mail envelope and tossed it into her outbox. A creature of habit, she'd clear that out later, around four.

"Can I come in?"

Megan glanced up, seeing none other than Joe Jacobsen, the company founder and CEO standing at the entrance to her cubicle. A small knot of nerves clenched and she took a breath to calm herself.

"Why, of course, Mr. Jacobsen. I was just finishing up the Montana report."

"Good, good. Come sit down, and call me Joe. Everyone does."

Everyone perhaps but her. Megan tried not to appear too flustered as he took a seat at the small table, which was really no bigger than a card table.

"So I bet you wonder what brings me by," he said.

Megan folded her hands into her lap to keep them from twitching. "Actually, I'll admit that I do, although in the year that I've worked for you, I've discovered you do wander your company and pop in on people all the time."

"Keeps them on their toes and I learn more that way," Joe said. "Sometimes it's good, sometimes it's bad, but it keeps the company humming."

"It's a good company," she said, mentally kicking herself for how lame and obvious that sounded. Joe Jacobsen didn't seem to notice.

"Of course it's a good company. I've been building it all my life. Now, as my delightful wife, Henrietta, reminds me, it's time to start looking toward the future. Not that I'm planning on retiring, mind you. I'm nowhere ready to do that. But what I am doing is starting a new program called Jacobsen Stars. Let me tell you about it."

Megan listened in fascination as he began to outline the entire program. A flicker of hope began inside her, and bloomed fully as he said the magic words. "I'm going around personally inviting people to participate in the program. You, Megan, have been chosen. What do you say?"

"Yes," she managed to stammer out. Then her voice became stronger. "I absolutely would be delighted to participate."

And she was. This was the opportunity of a lifetime, the type of opportunity she'd been slaving for when she'd put in all those years in night school earning her MBA. Her mother and Bill would be so proud.

"Of course, there is a little glitch," Joe said. His blue-eyed gaze caught hers, and something about the tone of his words brought her back down a little to reality.

"A glitch?"

"A glitch," Joe repeated. "Right now you are without a mentor." He sighed and ran his finger thoughtfully against his white beard. "With your credentials and talent I want someone perfect, someone who can bring out the best in you. And I've found just that person."

Lyle McKaskill, Megan thought. The fifty-year-old man was a wizard in the company, and she'd love to pick his brain. He'd forgotten more than she'd ever learned. Maybe the glitch was that Lyle's wife was having surgery in a month. Lyle would be taking family medical leave to be with her.

Grandpa Joe leaned back in the chair and folded his hands. "But don't despair. I have to admit I did spring the Jacobsen Stars program on him. Thus I expect that my grandson Harry will see the light in a day or two and agree to be your mentor."

"Harry?" The word, said in absolute appalled disbelief, came forth from her lips before she could bite it back. Please let her have heard Joe Jacobsen wrong.

Not Harry Sanders. Harry hated her. He'd never seemed to like her, and ever since that meeting a year ago—when she'd questioned the validity and rationale of his ideas—he'd made it perfectly clear that he'd fire her the first moment he could.

"Harry," Joe confirmed without noticing Megan's

stunned silence. "Now don't take it personally, but Harry turned down the idea of being your mentor. It has nothing to do with you; he's just a little bogged down with this New York merger, the chain of Evie's Pancake Houses that we're bringing under the Jacobsen Enterprises umbrella."

Joe paused before continuing. "Harry has agreed to think about it, but if he can't work you in, then I'm going to find a replacement mentor for you. However, let me be frank, I really don't want to consider that as an option except as a last resort. I've learned in business that when you know a decision you've made is the right one, you stick with it."

Megan forced the smile to remain on her face. So there it was. Joe Jacobsen had handpicked his grandson Harry Sanders to be her mentor. The joy that had originally seeped through Megan had ebbed fully. Then she drew herself up. Lemonade from lemons. If Harry wouldn't do it, Joe Jacobsen was prepared to find her another mentor. She'd hope for that.

"Anyhow, the program won't officially start for two weeks. That should give me plenty of time to convince Harry to change his mind. You two could really benefit each other."

Right. Of course they could. The only benefit Megan could see for Harry is that he could be one step closer to finding reasons to have her fired. As for her, the benefit to her career could be summed up in four words: nada, nothing, zero, zilch.

Joe reached for Megan's personal copy of the Montana report that she'd placed earlier in the middle of her table. "You know, I thought of sending Harry to Montana once," Joe said. "Then I wondered what he'd do with all that fresh air. He's such a city boy. Never wants to stray far from home. But he loves this company, I'll say that for him. Don't worry, Megan. He'll just need a little convincing to be your mentor, that's all. In fact, why don't you pay him a little visit today? He never leaves until five, and perhaps if you go personally and tell him how excited you are about having him mentor you, he'll understand how important I think this is."

Megan managed a faint smile. She'd go visit Harry all right, but only to convince him to back down so that someone else would have to be her mentor. Now there was a plan. "I could do that."

"Good." Joe stood, his business suit hardly wrinkled. She wondered how he managed to do that. Within an hour of arriving at the office, her conservative blue suit had crumpled from simply sitting in her chair and doing her work.

Joe Jacobsen gave her a big encouraging smile. "You'll find the complete Jacobsen Stars program in a package that will be delivered to you tomorrow morning. I'm glad to have you on board. Have a good afternoon, Megan."

Megan watched him go. Then a thought hit her. She poked her head out the cubicle and started after his retreating figure. "Mr. Jacobsen!"

He stopped and turned. She caught up to him. "What if Harry refuses and you can't find someone else? Am I out of the program?"

Joe gave her a reassuring look. "Oh no. I'll find you someone. But don't worry. I just know Harry will agree." He turned and walked away.

As Megan stared at Joe Jacobsen's retreating back, determination stole over her. She didn't want Harry Sanders as her mentor probably any more than he wanted her as his protégée. So all she had to do was convince him that it was in his best interest to say no. She went back to her cubicle to begin rehearsing her speech.

GRANDPA JOE WHISTLED as he stepped into the executive elevator. He pushed the button for the twenty-fifth floor. Whereas most corporate headquarters went skyward, Jacobsen Enterprises had sacrificed height for width. Although this was the main building, the complex sprawled several city blocks. It was one of the most valuable pieces of real estate in the city.

Not that he'd want a tall building anyway. He hated elevator rides. The trip to the top of the Sears Tower in Chicago, even though under two minutes, had about done him in. And to think he was a combat veteran.

He stepped out on his floor, and headed toward Andrew's office. Then thinking twice, he bypassed it. He loved his son-in-law as much as his own son, Blake, but unlike Blake, Andrew thought Grandpa Joe was a constant meddler. Perhaps he was, Grandpa Joe conceded, but after all he was so good at it. Andrew's marriage to Lilly was a perfect example, as was Darci and Cameron's.

Megan and Harry were next. He'd watched each for almost the past year. They were perfect for each other. They'd just have to figure it out and needed a nudge in the right direction. He'd given them that nudge, although honestly he knew they'd need more than just one. He glanced at his Rolex, a gift from his wife on their fortieth anniversary. Right now Megan should be on her way to Harry's office.

How Grandpa Joe wished he could be a fly on the wall for that conversation. He didn't expect it to go well, but that was okay. He had quite a few aces left to play.

HARRY KNEW MEGAN MacGregor had arrived before she even knocked on his office door. He'd been expecting her since that morning, and it hadn't made his lunch sit well. He hated to wait, especially for one as sneaky and conniving as Megan.

The subtle floral fragrance of her perfume reached him as she approached. His nose wrinkled as his brain registered the pleasant scent. Harry steeled himself. It was imperative that he remain in control of the situation. Thus, he deliberately chose not to look away from the e-mail he was reading on the computer screen. "A bit tardy, aren't you? Come to bring me the Montana report? It is complete, isn't it?"

Her tone hid her defensiveness well, but he still heard the echo of it. "Yes, as a matter of fact it is. Early, I might add. I put your copy into interoffice mail. I'm sure you'll receive it tomorrow."

Harry knew she stood right on the other side of his

desk. "And let's cut to the chase. As for tardy, I don't know what you're talking about," she said.

Harry turned around from his computer and took a moment to study her. Deliberately he ran his gaze up and down her figure, taking in the rumpled blue suit, the plain white cotton shirt that revealed nothing, not even the swell of her breasts.

He'd guess she wore sensible pumps, but he couldn't tell because his desk blocked his view of her feet. Even her brown hair was conservative, a short cut that framed her face. He returned his gaze to connect with hers. Despite a slight telltale flush that indicated that she hadn't liked his perusal, her haughty expression hadn't changed.

But she was flushed. Good. He liked that he had an effect on her. Whereas she might be able to fool everyone else, he was one man that could see right through her pretenses. While she might be pretty in an Ivory-soap sort of way, she definitely was not nice or pure.

"No, you're right," he said as he began his verbal offensive. "As for being tardy, you may not know what I'm talking about. Let me see if I can fill you in. Joe Jacobsen. Jacobsen Stars. Me not mentoring you even if my life depended on it." He watched her expression turn angry. "I expected you early this morning."

She placed her hands on her hips. "Your grandfather just came to see me a half hour ago to tell me about the program."

"Ah, that explains it. I'm surprised he didn't hit

you first thing in the morning. I guess he's slipping. But let me see if I've got the rest correct. You're here because he told you I'm not planning on being your mentor. Don't even bother trying to convince me otherwise.''

Megan gave a mock laugh. "Since we've already cut to the chase, let me continue to follow suit. As if I want you to be my mentor. Do I have a tattoo marked Desperate on my head? If so, tell me, I need to have it removed.''

Harry clapped his hands together and laughed. Quick on the comeback. He liked that. But of course, so was he. His lips pursed together before he spoke. "Score one for Megan. Tell you what though—" Harry gestured with the back of his hand toward the open door "—why don't you close that before you embarrass yourself. You'd hate for everyone to hear what you're really like.''

"What I'm really like?" Megan walked to the door. Harry caught a brief vision of Peggy's surprised face as Megan shut the door with a decisive click. "Now that we're alone, Harry Sanders, why don't you explain to me just what you are talking about?''

"I'm sure you know exactly what you are really like, which means that I have nothing to explain to you," Harry said. He'd been rehearsing this all day, and it was actually going quite well. "Let me just say that your entry into the Jacobsen Stars program is not one of my grandfather's better ideas.''

"You just wish you could fire me like you threatened to do.''

Now *there* was a good idea. Too bad she was Grandpa Joe's pet. Harry shrugged as if the issue was of little concern. "Someday I will."

Megan gave a haughty laugh. "Maybe if you ever get promoted you might get a chance. Of course, if the day ever comes that you get promoted, I'm sure I'll want to find another job before you run the company into the ground."

"Oh, you've taken the gloves off, haven't you, Megan? I wondered if you would. So since you're here, let's get down to why you came in the first place. You want me to refuse to be your mentor so that my grandfather chooses someone else for you. Not going to happen. He's not going to change his mind, and neither will I."

"What?!" Her mouth dropped open.

He arched an eyebrow. "Did I stutter? It's not going to happen."

She gestured wildly for a moment. "Are you insane? Look at us! We can't stand each other. You've done nothing but pick apart my performance since I got here a year ago. I'm sorry. Well, no I'm not. You made yourself look foolish in that meeting, Harry, not me."

Perhaps, but that didn't matter. He'd forgotten how intense she could be when angry. He shoved that intriguing thought aside. He had to stay focused.

"That meeting long ago is irrelevant. You are not good for Jacobsen, Megan. You are not a good fit for this company. But since it is not my company until such time that my grandfather and my father both step down and retire, I have little say in the matter.''

This was going better than he thought. He knew she'd come in prepared to fight, to prove they were incompatible. She'd played right into his hands. Megan drew herself up and leaned over his desk. ''So step aside and let me have a different mentor.''

''No. You know what they say about your past mistakes coming back to haunt you, don't you, Megan? That was your mistake, messing with me when you first came to work for Jacobsen Enterprises.''

''I did no such thing as what, messing with you? I came here on a professional basis. You and I may not be able to stand each other, but we can be professional. Why don't you just step aside so we can get past this issue and move on with our lives.''

She drew a deep breath, as if trying to calm herself. The movement made her breasts press forward. The suit jacket gaped open. She was wearing white lace.

Harry's throat went dry, and his next words simply disappeared. What was it about a clue train, or conversation train, or something like that derailing? He felt poleaxed. Come on! From seeing catalogs to actually removing women's clothing during lovemaking, he'd certainly seen lace-covered breasts before. But something about Megan and lace had just caused him to come unglued.

He blinked in order to yank his gaze away from staring at her breasts. He'd totally lost where he was, oh yeah, his office. And what he was saying or about to say? To regain control he stood, his six-foot-two height towering over her by six inches.

"I told my grandfather I'd make my decision soon. Who knows, maybe I just will be your mentor. After all, you're right. I need to be professional about this."

"You are such a, you are…"

"Oh spit it out, Megan. You can do better than that. Everyone knows how you enjoy making me look foolish. No one else is listening or even here. You don't have to pretend to be perfect. Let the real you hang out for once."

She tossed a hand though her short hair as if she was trying to regain control, and then the words spit forth. "You are a cad!"

Harry laughed. Boy, was she cute when she was angry. "Bravo. Impressive. You could have called me so much worse."

"You are impossible!" Her brown eyes flashed venom at him.

"Yes," he said. "I am. I take pride in that attribute."

"This was a waste of time." Megan strode over to the door, giving Harry a view of her shoes: plain, sensible blue pumps that matched her suit.

But she had nice ankles. Nice, thin, and not too bony. Just about perfect.

He stared at those perfect ankles as she stormed out of his office, her brown hair tossing around her head.

Peggy suddenly hovered at the doorway. "You got a call from Peters in New York while Ms. MacGregor

was here. I didn't want to disturb you and send it
through.''

"Thanks, Peggy. Ms. MacGregor is disturbing
enough. Go ahead and redial him for me, won't
you?''

"Certainly." Peggy went back to her desk.

Harry sat back down, surprised to find himself so
oddly invigorated. Megan *was* disturbing.

Arguing with her, how to describe it? The thought
that it had been better than some of the sex he'd ever
had, and man had he had some sex, came into his
mind. She was feisty, mind-blowing, difficult, tem-
peramental, and yet she faced him down and went
where most men would even fear to tread. Hmm.

She was an intriguing woman. No wonder men
found her a siren. Maybe he should be her mentor
just to spar with her again. It had been the most fun
he'd had in several weeks.

He laughed at the foolishness of that idea as Peggy
sent the call through.

Chapter Two

"Megan? Is that you?"

"It's me." Megan's purse landed with a thump on the side table. She took a moment to calm herself down. The meeting with Harry still had her totally keyed up.

The look on his face! Never in her life had she wanted to slap someone as much as she had wanted to smack Harry Sanders. Heck, she'd have kissed him if it would have given her back the control she'd lost in that meeting.

Of course, kissing him... Control. Harry always made her so furious, mostly at herself for being so unprofessional and out of control.

She strode into the living room of the shotgun flat she shared with her mother down in the area of Saint Louis known as the Hill. Her mother, propped up by pillows, was watching the evening news. Megan leaned and kissed her on the cheek. "How are you feeling today?"

Barbara MacGregor smiled weakly. "Okay. Today

is much better than yesterday," she said. "I'm not as numb in my legs as I was."

"Then that's good news," Megan said. She pushed the wheelchair aside and took a seat next to her mother. "Maybe the medicine is working."

"I hope so," Barbara said, her face clouding for a moment. Megan felt the familiar pang shoot through her. Her mother, the bravest woman she knew, did not deserve to have a primary-progressive case of multiple sclerosis. It had left Barbara needing a wheelchair most of the time. While her mother could still walk, her muscles were so weak that she used the wheelchair mostly to conserve precious energy.

"You just missed Bill. He brought me dinner before he went in to work." Barbara mentioned her fiancé of the past year. "He's tending bar tonight."

Ironically, her mother's fiancé, a wonderful retired gentleman with lots of spare time on his hands, worked for mad money at Henrietta's, Jacobsen's five-star, five-diamond restaurant.

Located only a few blocks away on Southwest Avenue, Bill often brought Barbara gourmet carryout dinners since she rarely left the house herself except for a doctor's appointment. It was just too much effort to go anywhere besides the general area of her home.

"So how was work?"

If one forgot about Harry Sanders, it was, "Great," Megan answered. "Mr. Jacobsen came by to tell me about a new program he's launching in two weeks called Jacobsen Stars. He wants me to participate."

"Honey! That's fantastic! Congratulations."

"Thanks," Megan replied as she told her mother about it, except of course, about Harry.

"I'm so proud of you," her mother said. She moved her hand slowly and finally covered Megan's. "You're the best daughter I could have asked for."

"Mom," Megan said. Tears brimmed in Megan's eyes and she bit her lower lip to keep from crying.

Barbara's voice suddenly sounded weary. "You shouldn't be having to take care of me, Megan. I'm only fifty. I should be fine."

A lump lodged in Megan's throat. She tried to lighten the moment. "Well, set a date with Bill and I'll pass you off on him."

Her mother's features clouded. "You know I can't do that. He's been too terrific and I can't take advantage of him. I'm thinking of calling off the engagement. He needs a woman who can get around, not one that is bedridden."

"Mom! He loves you!"

"Sometimes love isn't enough." A tear went down Barbara's cheek. Megan reached for a tissue and wiped it away.

Her mother was referring to Megan's father, who had dumped Barbara when she'd first been diagnosed with MS fifteen years ago. Barbara smiled brightly, as if the matter was concluded.

"Oh, I almost forgot," her mother said. "There's some dinner for you too. Bill even brought you some of that five-layer chocolate suicide cake you love so much."

"He's going to make me fat. I'll split it with you,"

Megan said. She rose to her feet. "In fact, I think I'll go get it and eat it first."

"You're not fat," Barbara called after her. "Girls who are five-foot-eight like you need a few pounds on them or they look too scrawny. But you are perfect. Any man would be thrilled to have you."

Maybe, until they learned that her mother came with the package. Not many men wanted to date her after discovering her invalid mother lived with her.

Personally, though, after seeing how Bill loved her mother, Megan wanted no part of any shallow, superficial man either. So, in essence, she'd given up dating. Right now, working at Jacobsen Enterprises and supporting her mother were much more important priorities.

Megan went into the tiny kitchen and took the carryout container from the refrigerator. She lifted the lid, her mouth watering at the sight of five layers of chocolate cake with milk chocolate frosting sandwiched between each layer. A dark chocolate frosting, sprinkled with grated chocolate, covered the entire cake. Nestled in the corner of the white container was a small cup containing the special chocolate sauce.

As always, Henrietta's chef had been more than generous with the portion. Megan took out a fork. Nothing like chocolate to make a girl feel better. She took a bite and walked back into the living room. Delicious.

"No offense, Mom, but you need to keep Bill just so we can keep getting this cake."

"I guess he does have his uses." Megan heard the

love in her mom's voice, meaning that Barbara's early melancholy had lifted. She was one of the most up people Megan knew, but even her mother did get depressed occasionally. How she remained as chipper, after needing to sell her home and move in with her daughter, was beyond Megan. Her mother was her hero.

"So any idea who is to be your mentor?" her mother asked after Megan fed her a piece of cake.

Megan wished she could lie, but she'd never been able to, especially to her mother. "Harry Sanders."

Barbara looked impressed. "The grandson?"

"One and the same."

"You don't sound so thrilled about it."

"I'm not. He hates me." Megan filled her mother in.

Barbara ate another bite of cake. "Actually," she said finally, "I think he will be a perfect choice for you. If you can deal with him, then you can deal with anyone."

Her optimistic mother would see the silver lining. "As usual, you're probably right," Megan said. "I didn't think about it that way."

Barbara smiled. "Joe Jacobsen must really think you're special if he gave you his grandson as a mentor. I think you'll discover that this works out better than you had ever hoped."

Megan forked the last bite of cake into her mouth to keep from answering. That remained to be seen.

TWO WEEKS LATER Megan stepped out of her cubicle and one last time attempted to smooth the wrinkles out of her skirt. It was her best suit, but the stubborn wrinkle at midthigh refused to budge.

"Good luck," Cheryl, the floor receptionist, called as Megan stepped into the elevator that would take her upstairs and to her first executive-level meeting as part of the Jacobsen Stars program.

"Megan, welcome," Joe Jacobsen greeted her as she stepped off the elevator. "We're in the large conference room. Just follow Sally."

And Joe passed Megan off on Sally as he waited for the next person.

Megan made a quick mental note. This was why Jacobsen was one of the best places to work. It was class personified. Knowing each "Star" would probably be nervous, Joe Jacobsen had greeted them personally and then had his secretary show them to their respective seats. His foresight eliminated what could have been many awkward moments.

Sally showed Megan to a seat between Jill Benedict and Alan Dalen, other Jacobsen Stars. Harry was across the table from her. His eyes narrowed as she pulled her chair out. "Harry," she said as she sat.

"Megan," he acknowledged before he reengaged the executive sitting to his right. It was the first time she'd seen him since their ill-fated meeting two weeks ago.

"I'm too excited," Jill confided to Megan.

"I know. It's a great opportunity," Megan replied as Joe Jacobsen came to the head of the table.

"Welcome, everyone. I'm excited to announce that

this meeting marks the first of many for our new Jacobsen Stars. Today's session is a think tank on the acquisition of Evie's Pancake Houses that we are planning. The information is in the folders in front of you."

Like everyone else, Megan opened the folder and studied the pages as Joe Jacobsen kept talking. "We've run into a problem, though." Everyone turned their heads to look at their boss.

"We never went after this as a merger. Evie's is a privately held chain of ten restaurants in the New York City market. Most of their value is in the actual real estate of the buildings themselves. Anyway, we now have competition. Odyssey Holdings has come along and proposed a merger. Whereas we would have been refurbishing the restaurants and replacing the Evie's name, they've proposed to keep it. Thoughts?"

Conversation began flying as people began tossing out ideas. Megan half listened but at the same time she started to really study the portfolio in front of her. Evie's, named for the owner's wife, was only being sold because the owner wanted to retire and none of his children wanted the business. Whereas Jacobsen Enterprises wasn't offering any stock, just cash, Odyssey had proposed stock options in its company as well. Odyssey had also proposed to keep all the restaurants open.

"I think we need to offer them more money," Harry said. "After all, we only want half of the locations and the rest can be sold to recoup some of our initial investment. Several of the restaurants are actually not showing a profit anymore.''

Megan tapped her pen on the binder. She was missing something.

''That idea has merit,'' someone else said. ''Some of the neighborhoods are not experiencing urban renewal. We should get out while we can before property value drops further.''

Megan watched Harry nod his agreement, a strand of blond hair falling into his face. He pushed it back. ''Exactly what we should do,'' he said.

''But it's the wrong thing to do.'' The room got quiet and Megan realized she'd spoken her thoughts aloud.

''And just why is that? Do you have a reason to back your thoughts up?'' The words, of course, came from Harry.

Megan glared at him. She would not let him get to her. ''As a matter of fact, I do.''

She turned and directed her comments to where Joe Jacobsen sat. ''Mr. Jacobsen, Evie's is a chain of restaurants named after the owner's wife. It's her legacy. No amount of money is going to sway him. Sure he wants financial freedom for the rest of his life, but not at the expense of his wife. It would have been like Dave Thomas selling Wendy's and it suddenly being called Sandy's. You have name recognition. That comforts people. It's why travelers on highways often go to McDonald's instead of the truck stop. They know what they're getting.''

''And how is this important?''

Megan shot Harry another dirty look. Hopefully he'd get the message and keep his mouth closed, although she doubted it. "It would be like Grandpa Joe's Good Eats suddenly being called something else. Mr. Jacobsen, could you just give up Grandpa Joe's knowing it was going to be torn down or sold for something else?" She looked back at Joe Jacobsen. He looked thoughtful. "It was your very first business venture, the one that gave you the capital to launch Henrietta's and Jacobsen. It's the company cornerstone. Well, could you give it up? Sir?"

Grandpa Joe shook his head. "No, which is why I haven't even considered the option even though the land value has quadrupled. The restaurant is like a baby. It even predates my children." He leaned back in his chair, his blue gaze fixating on her as he waited for her reply.

"Exactly. I'm sure neither can Mr.—" she checked the folder "—Althoff. While he wants out, he also has a bond with these neighborhoods. It's a private company, not public. It has no stockholders but himself and people he chose to sell shares to."

"But what about the restaurants that are losing money?" Harry asked. "What proposal do you have for them?"

Megan tapped her pen on the folder again. "We need to see why they are losing money. Is it that the neighborhood is in decline? Maybe there is too much competition in the area. Maybe the factory has closed. That's research we need to do. We may be able to move an Evie's restaurant down the block a ways and discover that it becomes an overnight sensation in its new home."

"Can you prove that works?" Harry asked.

"Absolutely," Megan turned back to Harry. If looks could kill. She pressed on anyway. "Remember when the Chicken Clatch found it wasn't successful in Eureka's fast-food row? So the company closed the store and built one five miles west in Pacific. It's a runaway success. We need to consider these types of things before we up our offer, or decide to kill the Evie's name."

Joe Jacobsen signaled his approval by nodding. "Excellent thoughts, Megan. Those are points we need to consider. Keeping ten successful venues, even if we have to move some down the block as Megan says, would be more income to Jacobsen than five. Jill, will you look into those possibilities?"

"Yes, sir," Jill replied. "I'd be delighted."

"Good," Joe said. "Next item."

As his grandfather moved on to the next item, Harry wanted to spit. Perfect little Megan MacGregor. Even though a brainstorming meeting wasn't a competition, once again she'd bested him. He brushed aside the begrudging respect he had for her performance. Her performance didn't matter. His did.

Would his grandfather ever see him as a valid player? Harry fumed, hating himself for even taking a moment to wallow in self-pity. But after all, when had he been good enough? He'd gone to the wrong college, failed Grandpa Joe's indoctrination into the company—no way had Harry wanted to spend two weeks cooking in Grandpa Joe's Good Eats—and now he hadn't even had decent ideas in a brainstorming session.

Megan's ideas were dead on, and what miffed Harry was that they'd come from her, not him. If he didn't get his act together, despite his MBA and being family, he'd never get promoted to any type of vice president. Too bad he was too driven and actually wanted to work. If not, he could have just lived off his trust fund and been a playboy like his cousin Shane.

He suddenly realized he hadn't been paying attention to what was going on. Panic filled him and he tried to focus. The last thing he needed was to be caught off guard in a meeting. Thankfully everyone was still talking about the New York trip. Jacobsen Enterprises was sending a team in one week to hopefully finish and wrap up the negotiations with Smith and Bethesda, the legal firm representing Evie's Pancake Houses.

"And of course, Megan, I want you as part of the team."

The chair hit Harry in the back as he sat up. Megan had just been added to the negotiation team? He had missed something. He was leading the team, and his nemesis had just thorned her way into his side.

To conceal his irritation, Harry focused on an oil painting on the wall above Megan's head. Suddenly everyone began clapping. Great. Obviously not his day. Now what had he missed?

Something major from the way everyone was smiling at him. Harry smiled automatically, hiding his lack of a clue.

"Congratulations," someone said.

"What a great pairing," the executive to his right said. "You and Megan MacGregor. She's talent extraordinare. Think of what you two can accomplish."

"Thank you," Harry said. He glanced up at his grandfather. Grandpa Joe looked smug and instantly Harry knew what he'd missed. Grandpa Joe had just announced at the meeting that he, Harry, was Megan's mentor. His beloved grandfather had just caught him in a corner and used it to his advantage. There was no way Harry could retaliate or back out now. He was stuck. Grandpa Joe arched his white eyebrows at Harry, the movement and his twinkling blue eyes saying what words could not.

Harry had been had. He was stuck. He'd have to play along. His sister's words came into his head. They were the ones she'd often repeated when frustrated during her tenure at Jacobsen's, "If I didn't love Grandpa Joe."

His grandfather came over to his seat and leaned down to speak just so Harry could hear. "It's for your own good, and that of Jacobsen's. Keep that in mind. I will expect you to accomplish this with no problems."

"I understand," Harry replied. He watched his grandfather leave the conference room. Four years of acting in high school theater allowed Harry to keep his face schooled into a neutral mask that hid all of his raging anger.

His only consolation was that across the table Megan looked shell-shocked. And for once she was speechless as people began leaving the meeting, each telling her congratulations as they walked by.

"HOW'D IT GO?" Cheryl looked up from sorting the mail as Megan returned to her office.

"Great," Megan lied as she walked toward her cubicle. "Just great."

Normally she would stop and chat with Cheryl. As a co-worker, she liked Cheryl. Because of poor performance, Megan had needed to fire the previous receptionist.

"I'm glad it went great," Cheryl called after her.

Yeah, Megan thought. Most of the meeting had gone great.

The meeting had been going well, even after she'd made the major blunder of opening her mouth and blurting out her opinion of Harry's idea.

After all, the meeting had been a brainstorming and that's what think-tank brainstorming was, a shouting out of ideas so that people could look at all sides of the issues.

But she'd crossed Harry Sanders, again. Why did she keep doing that? This was the second time her politically incorrect semantics had discredited his ideas.

And then Joe Jacobsen announced to everyone that Harry was her mentor.

"I didn't accept the job, you know."

She'd recognize his voice anywhere. Its husky baritone washed over her, and she whirled around in her chair, finding Harry Sanders standing at the entrance to her cubicle, his presence filling the small opening. "So we can find some common ground and manage to work together on this project, know that he pole-axed me too."

"I see," Megan said. She bit back her anger. If he'd only backed out when she'd asked. But that didn't matter now. They were stuck. Fighting like at their last encounter in his office would do both little good.

So instead she took a good look at him. Tiny hints of strain etched lines around his blue eyes. They were Jacobsen blue eyes, just like his grandfather's. The only thing missing was the warmth Joe Jacobsen always had in his.

But there was no doubt about it, Harry Sanders was a beautiful man. His hair, almost the color of wheat with natural highlights washed through, was short and cropped into the latest fashion. His eyes were set deep—the top lid hidden, sunken into his face like Paul Newman's or Simon Baker's. And his lips, Megan didn't want to think about those, or the number of women they'd kissed. Everyone at Jacobsen knew Harry's playboy reputation. While he never dated anyone at work, the switchboard fielded enough of his calls, more than triple anyone else's.

He smiled suddenly, and it lit up his whole face. Laugh lines creased around those generous lips, and Megan sucked in her breath. If he looked like that when he smiled politely, what would he look like when he really smiled, smiled with pleasure or wanting?

That was dangerous ground she didn't need to tread. Harry Sanders was business, that was all. Averting her gaze from his straight white teeth, she tried to concentrate on what he was saying as he sat in a chair at her small table. Instead she saw paisley socks that perfectly matched both his suit and his shoes. The man knew how to dress. She blinked.

"...so my grandfather again gets what he wants. I'll expect you to have the full proposal read by tomorrow. Even though Jill is researching your ideas, you need to be certain she gives you a full report before you board the plane. And lastly, buy yourself an updated wardrobe. Those clothes need to go."

"What?" Had she heard him correctly? Her mouth opened a little in surprise.

"Clothes," Harry said without missing a beat. She had heard him correctly. "You look like a dowager duchess. Prim. Proper. Not quite the look we want. You're what, twenty-something?"

"Twenty-seven." Her voice was indignant.

"Right. Well you should dress sleek. Young. Professional. Not frumpy. We're going into the fashion capital of America and you aren't sixty."

"There is nothing wrong with my clothes," Megan repeated, reining in her anger. After all, her clothes were designer labels, she'd just found them in an upscale consignment shop.

Harry folded his hands into his lap and leaned forward. The movement allowed her to glimpse the muscles under the suit jacket and her mouth went dry. "I've been given the task of being your mentor. Why don't you assume I do know some things and follow my advice. Since I am your mentor, you are now a reflection of me and my tutelage. Thus, I'd prefer you listen."

He leaned back and put his hands behind his head. That movement emphasized other muscles. Megan resisted the urge to lick her lips.

What was it about him? Other men had sat in her cubicle, but why was Harry's presence affecting her like this? Megan attempted to focus, her gaze instead watching Harry as he shrugged, his jaw flexing as he spoke.

"But, if you don't want to update your wardrobe I suppose that's fine. When you discover I'm right, it will come at your expense."

She attempted to regain control of the situation. Harry Sanders, who always looked perfect, was in her cubicle telling her how to dress. The thought rankled, giving her some of the bite she needed. "I'll see what I can do. Anything else?"

Harry took what seemed like forever to study her. Megan felt her body heat as his blue-eyed gaze roved over her. It took all her mettle not to move a muscle. Whatever this test was, she would pass.

He finally spoke, his voice a bit lower, huskier, than before. "No. There's nothing else. Everything else, hair, makeup, is fine. Just fine. Make sure you lose the frumpy clothes. My sister usually shops at…"

He rattled off the names of some stores and then he was gone.

Megan stared at the empty chair. Had he really been there at all? She knew he had, but it seemed so improbable. Harry Sanders, extending an olive branch of sorts?

If that's what it actually was? And if it was an olive branch, it was probably only because he was stuck with her, and her with him. But he was correct about one thing. He did know how to dress, and he always looked impeccable no matter what designer suit he wore

New clothes. Buying clothes would break her tight budget, but as much as she hated to admit it, Harry was right. She needed a young professional wardrobe.

New York, here I come.

Chapter Three

Jacobsen Enterprises Internal Memo
From: Joe Jacobsen, CEO
To: Andrew Sanders, president
Re: Harry/Jacobsen Stars

The meeting went well. Of course, both Harry and Megan looked a little upset that neither got what they wanted, but they covered well. Both have learned that first rule in business, never let them see you cry. Anyhow, I'm sending Megan to New York with Harry. Her ideas in the meeting were fantastic, and a full transcript will be on your desk by tomorrow morning. J.J.

Jacobsen Enterprises Internal Memo
From: Andrew Sanders, president
To: Joe Jacobsen, CEO
Re: Harry/Jacobsen Stars

You truly are a crazy old coot. Do you really think forcing the two into some unhappy togetherness is

going to spark romance? You'll be lucky you get any type of merger out of this mess you've created.
A.S.

Jacobsen Enterprises Internal Memo
From: Joe Jacobsen, CEO
To: Andrew Sanders, president
Re: Harry/Jacobsen Stars

It's an acquisition, and of course everything will work out. I have a gift, a natural talent, for both business and romance. Want to bet on it? Didn't we say double or nothing on Harry?
J.J.

Jacobsen Enterprises Internal Memo
From: Andrew Sanders, president
To: Joe Jacobsen, CEO
Re: Harry/Jacobsen Stars

Here we go again.
A.S.

"LAST CALL FOR Flight 690 to LaGuardia."

"Here," Megan rushed up to the counter, her new designer blue Italian pumps already rubbing a blister on her heel. She handed the clerk her boarding pass and began digging for her driver's license.

So much for being on time for her flight. She'd left home late, traffic through the city on Highway 70 had been terrible, and the only long-term parking had been in lot A, the farthest one away.

To make matters worse, her gate in Lambert International's D-concourse had been all the way at the end, and she'd been practically running the whole way, including on the speed walks. It seemed that everyone had a flight out of the Saint Louis international airport at 8:00 a.m. on a Tuesday morning.

"Has your luggage been with you at all times?" the counter clerk asked.

"What? Oh yes," Megan said, snapping her attention to the task at hand, getting on the plane. Within moments she was walking down the gangway to the Boeing 757 for the 882 mile flight to New York.

This was her first time flying as a requirement of her job. She'd always known Joe Jacobsen refused to hire charter flights or even purchase his own jet, so it surprised her to discover that instead of coach, her seat was in first class. The few times she'd ever flown before had all been in coach where she was lucky to even get beverage service.

"Welcome," the flight attendant said as she took Megan's boarding pass. "Second row, which is actually the first one on your left, the aisle seat. You'll need to put your carry-on luggage under the seat. The overhead bins are full."

"Thanks," Megan said. She walked the few feet toward her seat.

"About time."

"Oh. You." Megan's breath exhaled into a sigh of resignation as she saw Harry. He was already seated by the window, a partially full glass of orange juice in his left hand.

"Hello to you too, seatmate. Let me tell you how delighted and excited I am to share this two-hour flight with you." His blue eyes narrowed. "But at least you followed my advice. New clothes. Nice."

Her new V-neck silk blouse gaped open as she attempted to shove her carry-on bag under the seat. She wrestled with keeping her shirt closed while she tried to shove the bag into the small space.

"New underthings too?"

Great. So much for success with her shirt. He'd been staring at her breasts. She covered her mortification by remaining flippant. "You said new clothes. I bought new everything."

She gave one last irritated shove and the carry-on bag slid into place. Her purse she shoved into the space in front of her. She took her seat and strapped herself in.

"Orange juice or V8?"

"Orange juice," Megan replied, taking the plastic cup the flight attendant handed her. She let the cold juice roll over her tongue. Just what she needed.

Harry's voice came out of nowhere. "I would have pegged you for a V8 girl. All those vegetables."

"You would peg me for a lot of things that I'm not," Megan said. She looked ahead at the wall in front of her. The fabric was an interesting pattern of blue. *Please don't let him be a chatty seatmate.*

"So tell me then about the real Megan MacGregor. You know, the things that aren't on your résumé."

"Most of them are none of your business." To her delight she realized that sitting in first class meant having an extra-wide armrest. At least she wouldn't need to jostle with Harry for that.

Next to her, Harry shrugged. "We have two hours to kill."

Megan heard the rumbling of the engine as the plane began to back away from the gate. "Didn't you bring a magazine? Business paperwork? My briefcase is in my carry-on. I have plenty to do."

"Like you'll be able to pull that out and get to it. 'Course, the show was pretty good."

She felt her face flush. There never was a dull moment with Harry, was there? "I have a magazine in my purse."

"Let me guess. *Vogue? Mademoiselle*?"

From his tone she knew he was poking fun at her. "For your information it's *U.S. News and World Report*. I also have a book."

His blue eyes twinkled. "A romance?"

"No, a mystery by Sue Grafton."

"Yeah, I didn't think it would be romance. Although with your prim-and-proper facade you could secretly harbor stacks of those sweep-me-off-my-feet historicals at home. You know, the ones with the half-naked guy on the cover."

"I do not," Megan retorted. She preferred contemporary romance, not that she'd tell him that.

"Do you even have a romantic bone in your body?"

"Harry!"

"She calls my name."

The plane began to accelerate down the runway,

thrusting them back into their seats. So engrossed in their conversation, they'd missed the security lecture. She made a mental note to remember where the exits were, something she'd been taught to do on an *Oprah* show on surviving disasters. But Oprah hadn't known about Harry Sanders. He could have been a show all by himself.

"It won't crash," Harry said as if reading her mind. "I've never had a bad flight."

Of course the golden boy wouldn't. The skies wouldn't dare misbehave for him. "Yes, but with my bad luck, today might be the first. Look at the proof. We got stuck with each other, didn't we?"

He smiled, giving her the grin that she knew had melted hearts for miles. "The more I think of that, the more I think how lucky you are, in the good sense. I'm a Jacobsen."

"So? That just means you got your foot in the door. Personally, I would have rather had Lyle McKaskill."

"Really? He's fifty. But then, I forget you like them older." Harry's smile had faded.

"What's that supposed to mean?"

But the plane had launched itself into the air, and, instead of answering, Harry turned his attention out the window as the city of Saint Louis began fading from view.

Megan fumed. Dig and rip. What did he mean anyway with that crack? Did he know how absolutely infuriating he was? He was a cad. A jerk. A first-class… Mentally she ripped on him, but it did nothing to assuage the conflicting feelings now going through her.

She'd always avoided being this close to Harry Sanders. The man was a walking pheromone, a womanizer. And she wasn't as immune to him as she'd always thought she was. Sitting next to him she could smell his cologne. He smelled of wilderness, of something wild and primal. His short blond hair looked silken, eminently touchable. She could picture running her hands into the golden strands, and grabbing hunks of his beautiful hair as he thrust into her. She'd pull his lips back down to hers and...

Stop right there! That was not a picture or a fantasy she needed. The last thing she needed was to have any type of sexual harassment charges drummed up on her, or for her to send any sort of subliminal sexual messages to Harry.

The man was one hundred percent pure playboy. He ran through women like water.

The last thing she needed was to lose her focus. Harry Sanders was, for better or worse, her mentor. This was business. That was all. Her career could be made or broken on this trip. She couldn't screw it up with thoughts she didn't need to be having about Harry Sanders.

HARRY WATCHED Saint Louis fade into the ground below. They'd gone westward, and then circled back, heading east over the northern end of the city on their way to New York. From his seat by the window he was able to look southward and see the Gateway Arch as the plane cut through the scattered remnants of high cirrus clouds. It was a beautiful day for flying.

So focused on his thoughts, he barely heard the captain's announcement that they'd reached their cruising altitude of thirty-something thousand feet. Had it been thirty-two or thirty-four? Maybe it had been thirty-six. The ground could be seen intermittently. He thought about asking the flight attendant for a moment, but then dismissed that idea. There was no point.

He knew the damage to his psyche and concentration was already complete. The irritating Megan MacGregor had wormed her way under his skin.

He couldn't believe it when she'd almost missed the plane, and worse, he had actually found himself worried about her! What was wrong with him? He'd been glad to see her! Her missing the plane would have been a godsend; she would have proven once and for all how irresponsible she truly was, and how she wasn't what she seemed. But she'd made it just in time.

And she'd taken his advice. She'd bought new clothes. The saleslady who'd helped her ought to be shot. Megan had gone from a prim, proper and frumpy man-eater to a sexy, irresistible siren in a blue suit. And underneath her silk deep-V shirt she'd worn cream-colored lace.

No man needed to see that, and Harry had been only inches from being able to bury his face right into the ripe breasts that the lace did nothing to conceal.

Thank goodness she hadn't gotten Lyle McKaskill

for her mentor. The man was married, but that wouldn't have stopped Megan. Harry winced slightly. No guy stood a chance, not even him.

Maybe Megan was the type that a man needed to sleep with once. Not that Harry planned on sleeping with her, of course, but he comforted himself on knowing what she'd be like—a quick fling. Then afterward he would discover that she wasn't worth it—that the fire was in the chase, not the capture.

But it was tempting. He'd told Grandpa Joe that Megan was a sexual harassment case waiting to happen. He had to make sure it wasn't with him.

"Are you going to explain your comment from earlier?"

Her voice cut through the haze of his thoughts and he turned to face her. She sat a scant eighteen or so inches from him. To kiss her, all he'd have to do was lean over. "What comment?"

She sighed, her full red lips puckering with mild distaste. "Never mind. Perhaps we should discuss the upcoming meetings. Why don't you give me your thoughts on what we're up against."

"I could," Harry said, and then he drew himself up. "Why not?"

After all, they did have two hours to kill. He proceeded to fill her in. She listened attentively, her expression never changing as he outlined the new Jacobsen Enterprises strategy.

"Who came up with that?" she asked.

"Jill Benedict and Alan Dalen. If you want to discuss the presentation with them, they're right behind us, three rows back, right before the partition. Their mentors are seated across from them. Aisle five.''

"No. I don't need to talk to them." The shake of Megan's head sent her brown hair into her face. She pushed the loose strands behind her ears. Along with her new clothes, she'd gotten her hair cut. Harry resisted the urge to tuck a wayward strand back behind her right ear. Her face scrunched into cute ridges across her forehead, indicating she was deep in thought.

"You don't like the idea," Harry observed.

Megan gestured. "No, I don't. It's still limited. It's missing something.''

"Jill researched everything you discussed at the meeting. You remember the meeting."

Megan sidestepped that question as if that meeting was now irrelevant. "I should have done the research on this myself. I hate delegating. Something's always missing whenever I do.''

"Nothing's missing. It's a great plan. Betty is going to do the presentations. We'll be meeting in the conference room of Smith and Bethesda, the legal firm that Evie's hired to act as intermediaries for the sale. It's as close to neutral ground as we can get. Evie's legal team, and some representatives from Evie's, will be there.''

"The presentation is still wrong. It's missing something,'' Megan repeated. Her face still showed her concentration. She took a sip of juice.

"You said it was missing something in the meeting too,'' Harry reminded her. "We've fixed that.''

"No, we haven't. We've simply found out why the restaurants were losing money, and that the problems that they're having are easily correctable. We can keep the establishments open, which eliminates one of Evie's complaints against our bid. But we didn't address Evie's main concern. What is it that makes our presentation better? Why are we a better company than Odyssey Holdings? Why should they sell to us instead of merge with Odyssey?"

Harry looked at Megan. Her face had become more animated, and he found his gaze drawn to her full lips as she spoke. Those lips were eminently kissable. "What makes Jacobsen better, Harry?"

"Grandpa Joe." The words were the first thing to his mind and they shot off his tongue before he even thought to think about and perhaps stop them.

"Exactly!" Megan looked triumphant. "That's it! Grandpa Joe, well, to me, Joe Jacobsen. He's what we need to sell to Evie's. Grandpa Joe cares. That's what makes us better than Odyssey Holdings, why Evie's should take our bid over Odyssey's. Jacobsen Enterprises is a family company. Sure, it's a public company with publicly traded stock, but the family holds the majority of the stock. You've got a trust fund full of it, don't you?"

"That's irrelevant."

"Harry…" Her tone protested his vague answer. "This is important."

He exhaled. He'd been raised not to talk about how much money he had. "Only thirty percent of the stock is owned by nonfamily members."

"Evie's is a private company, based on a man's love for his wife. What we need to sell, Harry, is your family. Your family firm will take care of Evie's. It won't be lost somewhere in the corporate shuffle of some large, anonymous holding company. Jacobsen will take care of Evie's, just like it was a Grandpa Joe's Good Eats.''

Harry thought about that for a moment. She had a point. An excellent point, in fact. ''I'll have Betty work it into the presentation.''

''No.'' Again Megan's firm tone stopped him. ''She's not going to make the presentation. You are.''

''What? That's not my role on the team. While it's under my leadership, Betty is a better presenter.''

''It doesn't matter. You are going to present the proposal, Harry. Look at the image you'll bring to the floor. Grandpa Joe cares about this acquisition so much that he sent his grandson, a stockholder, to personally oversee it. You need to make the presentation, and run the negotiations. You're not the new car manager but the salesman on the floor. I'll help.''

Harry wasn't sure he liked this idea. His sister Darci had always been the negotiator. Even Kyle, Alan's mentor, was a much better negotiator than Harry was. Harry always handled the public relations end of things, the spit-polish so to speak. He calmed nerves, smoothed over ruffled feelings, made transitions flawless. As Megan had just put it, he was the new car manager. He cemented the deals but was never in the forefront.

''And how will you help?'' he asked.

"I'm going to write your presentation." Megan reached into her purse and pulled out a Palm Pilot. Within a moment she'd set up a little keyboard attachment to the unit and had the whole thing sitting on her fold-out tray. "It shouldn't be too hard. It's not like we have to redo any of our visual aids or acquisition folders."

"Breakfast," the attendant interrupted. She handed over a plate of what looked like bagels, bacon, and scrambled eggs.

"No, thanks," Megan said. "I ate already. But I'll take more orange juice when you have a moment."

"Certainly," the attendant said as she moved down the aisle.

Harry munched on a piece of bacon. Not too bad. Like Megan, he'd eaten earlier as well, but some snack food never hurt. They'd be starting the negotiation meeting at one, right after lunch. He spread some cream cheese and strawberry jam on the bagel, took a bite, and watched as Megan's fingers flew over the small keyboard. She'd just amazed him.

Maybe there was a little substance to her after all.

It wasn't as if he couldn't do the presentation, he just never had been the front man before. But with Megan writing the proposal, suddenly he felt confident. They could make a good team.

Strictly business, of course.

But she challenged him. She rubbed him raw. His grandfather's favorite phrase—as iron sharpens iron—came into his head.

He finished off the bagel and listened to her outline

her proposal. And then he grilled her within an inch of her life over it. She managed to hit each one of his concerns, diffuse them. "It's good," he finally said.

She smiled, and suddenly Harry needed to clench his right armrest. How easy it would have been to simply shift to his left, put his left hand on the back of her neck, bring her face to his and kiss her.

She's a siren. A siren who's engaged to a man twenty years her senior. That thought threw a bucket of cold water over him. Twenty years her senior. There was no way her engagement could be true love. Distaste filled Harry's mouth. But at least he and Megan had proven that they could work together. They could be a team. But that was probably all. He doubted they could even be friends.

"You know," Megan said, "I used to think you didn't know very much about business, but in reality you really do."

"I have an MBA that I did work for," Harry snapped. "I did graduate magna cum laude from Vanderbilt."

"I know. I'm sorry. Don't be so touchy. You're the grandson, though. Everyone knows you'll always have a job."

Maybe a job, and a trust fund, but Harry knew that because he was family the need to prove himself was even greater. Grandpa Joe was an eccentric where his family was concerned. He'd wanted both Harry and his sister Darci to be indoctrinated into the company by serving two weeks in every "aspect" of the company. Harry had drawn the line at being a cook at

Grandpa Joe's Good Eats. Darci, however, had survived her waitressing gig. Megan didn't know about Grandpa Joe's crazy indoctrination schemes into the family business, or that Grandpa Joe favored his granddaughters. Even Harry's cousin, Nick Jacobsen, who at twenty-seven headed the East Coast Jacobsen restaurant-supply business out of the Chicago office, only seemed to please Grandpa Joe about half of the time.

"Here's your juice." The flight attendant was back, pouring each of them refills from a clear plastic carafe.

Time to take a break. "I think we've covered enough business," Harry said to Megan as he passed the attendant his plate. He hadn't eaten the eggs. "We've got about another hour before we land. Why don't you read your book." He pulled the airline company magazine out of the seat pocket and opened it.

"Sure," Megan said. She folded up her keyboard and put her Palm Pilot away. Disappointment etched her features but Harry didn't notice.

For once Megan was glad that Harry's nose was buried deep in the magazine. She didn't need him reading her current thoughts. Her opinion of him had definitely gone up.

Well, not much, but definitely a change for the better. She'd always viewed Harry as an alpha male, but never as a skilled alpha male businessman. While Harry certainly looked the part of a businessman, in her opinion he had never before acted the part. In her presence he'd always been cutting, perhaps even bordering on cruel. His actions and business lore had never inspired her to greatness, nor had any of his ideas. His ideas, at best, had been lame and textbook.

But today Harry had grilled her, and each question had been dead on, deliberate, and designed to make her push herself and her ideas further. She'd felt herself blossoming under his tutelage, and in pushing herself she'd also seen Harry adapt and push himself as well.

Maybe Joe Jacobsen had been right in selecting Harry to be her mentor. Maybe they would both learn something in the process.

But an unresolved question nagged at the back of her mind. Would she be safe with Harry as her mentor? For wasn't he every woman's fantasy, and she had to admit it, even her own?

Maybe that's why she disliked him so much. The man was sex personified. A woman couldn't help herself around him. Megan didn't even want to think about what touching him would feel like. She couldn't let herself have that fantasy, the one of running her fingers over his bare chest and thus finding out if light blond hair dusted it, or if the muscles instead were silky smooth.

No, even if there weren't laws against her sudden wantonness, for she knew that Harry would never want her back, getting involved with Harry was a dumb idea period. She wasn't from his world. She had a public school education and MBA, and she hadn't graduated with any honors. She hadn't won the genetic lottery with her family the way he had. She buried herself in Sue Grafton's *P is for Peril* the rest of the flight.

"WHAT DO YOU mean we have adjoining rooms?" At approximately 9:00 p.m. Megan's voice rose above the crowd milling in the hotel lobby, and several people turned to look at her.

"Keep your voice down!"

Megan closed her mouth, realizing her social gaffe the moment Harry had hissed his response at her. She looked around, seeing the interested looks crossing the faces of the four other members of the Jacobsen Enterprises team. Harry had just checked everyone into the Marriott East Side hotel, and had pressed an electronic passkey into her hand.

The afternoon meetings at the Smith and Bethesda offices had gone well, and now at 9:00 p.m. the team was finally checking in. "We have a suite," Harry announced for everyone's benefit. "You are in a room on one side, I am in a room on the other. Everyone will meet in the living area of the suite at eight tomorrow morning for a strategy meeting before we go back to Smith and Bethesda." He rattled off a suite number. "Other than that, everyone is free until then."

And with that, people scattered, leaving Megan standing in the ornate lobby with Harry. "How could you do this to us?"

"Do what?" Harry peered over at her as if she were crazy. Megan's face flushed. "I didn't make the arrangements, and no one would have thought twice about them if you hadn't just yelled at the top of your lungs. For a woman of your worldly talents, you'd have thought you could handle something like a suite. And you call yourself a professional business-woman?''

He was right, and Megan hated herself for it. She'd learned in business school to keep her personal feelings hidden. She'd learned to be calculated. But she'd never mastered being cold, and she'd been seeing Harry differently ever since the plane. He'd been nothing short of phenomenal in the meetings that afternoon, and afterward he'd led the team quickly through the dinner debriefing at Jacobsen's Manhattan restaurant.

She didn't need to share a suite with Harry Sanders. She wasn't seeing him anymore as just an evil monster, the devil incarnate. Instead she was beginning to see him as a man, as a human being. That was not good. She could not afford to lose her focus.

Living close to him was going to be pure torture. It was a complication she didn't need. A bellhop carried their luggage and within moments had explained how the doors operated. Each bedroom was a standard hotel room operated by its own key.

An adjoining door, typical to hotel rooms, opened into the center living area of the suite. That area, the size of two hotel rooms, contained a conference table for eight, a small wet bar and a living area with a huge big-screen TV. Both keys operated the main door to the suite.

"Your suite has a terrace," the bellhop said as he showed them the sliding glass doors. Megan stepped out onto the terrace as Harry tipped the man for his service. Part of the brick terrace was covered, and it was large enough for potted plants and patio furnishings. Megan looked around, taking in the fact that some people were still working in the buildings around her. From the street below a car horn blared.

"A little less nervous now?"

Harry's breath was warm on her neck and she started. His chuckle was low against her ear. "Sorry, Megan, you aren't worth jail time. I won't toss you over."

"That's good to know," Megan responded, deliberately keeping her voice light and carefree as she turned around to face him. Her breath caught in her throat. All she had to do was fully extend her arms and she'd be touching him.

"I'm going to watch a movie. We've got cable, and pay-per-view. You can join me if you want. I'm sure there's something on that we'll both like."

And there was the full olive branch.

But should she take it?

Megan stared at Harry. He'd taken off his suit coat and had shed the tie. He'd rolled up the white shirtsleeves, cuffing them midway before his elbow. Golden hair dusted his forearms, and having to know, Megan's gaze moved to discover that smooth skin peeked out from where Harry had unbuttoned the top two buttons of his shirt.

She swallowed, hard, glad that the brick wall of the

terrace supported her and kept her from staggering.
She did not need to spend any more time than nec-
essary in the magical proximity of Harry Sanders.
''I'm tired,'' she managed to say.

It must be a trick of the light that flickered between
the buildings surrounding the hotel. Harry looked disappointed, but Megan knew that couldn't be right.
''I'm going to get some sleep,'' she said.

He stepped back, away from her, giving her the
room to move past him. ''Suit yourself. You would
be the girl who needs sleep in the city that never
sleeps.''

''That's me,'' she quipped, stepping into the cooler
interior of the suite. She called back over her shoulder, ''Besides, I have to unpack.''

Which of course took her only five minutes. What
an absolutely lame excuse.

She gazed around her hotel room. No cramped
space here, it easily held the furnishings—a king-size
bed, a chair and ottoman, a desk with computer ports,
and the dresser she'd neatly put her clothes into. The
rest of her clothes were hanging in the closet. She
could do some work on her computer, but there was
really nothing pressing. She heard the muted sounds
of the television in the other room.

You're a chicken, her reflection in the mirror said.
Brown eyes gazed at each other.

A wise chicken, Megan retorted. I don't need to
get involved with Mr. Love 'em and Leave 'em in
the other room, no matter how sexy he is. I have to
remember my future, my mother and the expensive

medicines she needs. I need to stay away from Harry Sanders. I need to keep myself professionally distant. He's a Jacobsen; he could break my career.

Her reflection showed the doubt on her face. But he's invigorating. Look at our conversation on the plane. Look at the presentation he did. Maybe you are wrong about him.

Maybe I'm not. Megan closed her eyes for a moment, shutting out the woman in the mirror. Even the darkness, though, didn't give her the respite she wanted.

Instead, pictures of her and Harry appeared like erotic images on a movie screen. She could see herself running her hands over Harry's bare chest, caressing and stroking his smooth muscular skin. She could see him leaning in, bringing those full lips down to kiss her. She could see herself fisting her hands into his short blond hair. And when he fingered underneath the silky V of her shirt...

"I need to stay away from Harry Sanders." Megan repeated the words, this time aloud, as if hearing them spoken loudly cemented her resolve and somehow silenced the reflection in the mirror that thought otherwise.

She quickly formed a plan. I'll let him have his moment in the sun. I'll keep quiet, maintain just a simple business relationship. I'll not cross him. After all, he's a Jacobsen. He'll be a vice president no matter what, and if I want to be, I'm going to have to learn to work with him. Perhaps the best business tactic to use this time is to take the path of least resistance.

Her reflection said nothing, and Megan sternly gave herself one last firm look before reaching for her toothbrush. "I need to stay away from Harry Sanders," she repeated, jutting her chin forward as if daring her reflection, her innermost thoughts, to contradict her.

And since I don't like him, it should be easy. Right?

Chapter Four

By 8:30 a.m. during the conference in the suite, Harry didn't think anything of Megan's quiet behavior. By 10:00 a.m. at the presentation he was beginning to be worried. During the working lunch he was angry. And by 3:00 p.m. Harry Sanders was ready to kill Megan MacGregor. Never had a woman so infuriated him. And here he was, thinking that they were past all this!

But no, Ms. Night and Day had just pulled another one-eighty and totally changed the rules again. She'd barely said three words to him all day if you didn't count yes, no and good morning.

Just what was wrong with her?

Harry fumed. She was ruining the whole presentation and the meetings. Didn't she see that?

Obviously not as she laughed at something the young lawyer from Smith and Bethesda said. Harry leaned back in his chair and took a moment to study Megan as Jill presented some financial figures. He'd memorized the pie charts by heart this morning.

Megan wasn't even looking at the graphics, and

neither was the man next to her. Instead he was leaning over toward Megan, his preppy haircut letting a
swoop of dark brown angle across his face. Megan
had her head cocked to the side as he whispered
something in her ear. She nodded, smiled, and leaned
over to whisper something back to him.

Close, friendly behavior for two people who had
just met. Harry frowned and watched the scene play
out for a few more moments. Couldn't Megan see
what was going on? The man was hitting on her.
Surely she wasn't that naive.

A bitter taste filled his mouth. No, Megan wasn't
naive, and the afternoon was turning out just great.
Not only had the Jacobsen team not made the progress they needed, but Megan was carrying on with
one of the opposing counsel. The woman was a man-
eater.

"Harry?" Jill looked at him, and Harry came back
to attention. He needed to salvage at least something
out of this meeting. With Megan in silence, if one
didn't count the whispered conversation to the gigolo
next to her, gone was the dynamic that had driven the
Jacobsen train yesterday. The negotiations had de-
railed.

"Thanks, Jill." He fielded about a few hours'
worth of questions before both teams decided to call
it a day. It was almost 6:00 p.m. and negotiations
would begin the next morning at nine. Everyone began to file out of the conference room.

"We'll meet at eight tomorrow just like we did
today," Harry told his team. "Have a good night."

"I'll see you tomorrow then," the man who had been sitting by Megan was saying. Harry looked over to see Megan shoving some papers into her briefcase. "Tomorrow," Megan replied as the man left the room.

Did the woman not have any tact? Harry made an instant decision. "Megan, a word with you."

She looked at him in surprise. "Yes, Harry?"

"You and I need to talk." He controlled his tone.

"Is there a problem?"

She blinked, those brown eyes of hers looking so innocent. How he knew differently. His voice came out a bit harsher. "I'd say so."

Megan folded her arms across her chest. "Well, the room's empty. Go ahead."

"We aren't talking here." Harry moved forward and with his free hand cupped her elbow. A fire burned between her skin and his, and Harry attributed the electric sensation to his current state of agitation. "Get your briefcase. We'll talk over dinner."

"I need to work on—"

"You can work at dinner, Megan. Think of it as a job requirement, an order, if that helps your misguided sensibilities."

"I do not have misguided sensibilities. What are you talking about?"

"Like I said. Not here. We'll talk at dinner where we won't be disturbed." He propelled her into the elevator, glad to see that no one from either negotiating team was present. They rode down in silence, and within moments were in a cab headed to Jacobsen's Manhattan restaurant.

The hostess recognized them from the previous evening, and within moments they found themselves seated at a secluded table away from the hustle and bustle. Their waitress approached. "Scotch on the rocks and a glass of the Napa Riesling. Bring a starter of spinach and artichoke dip."

He turned to face Megan. She looked indignant. "What?"

"You just ordered for me," she said.

"So? It saves time. That's the wine you chose when we were here last night."

"Maybe I didn't want it again. You had no right to just order for me."

"I don't need a right," Harry retorted. He tamed his temper. Although he was angry, he'd never been one to fly off the handle and be irrational. "The way I figure it is this, if you have the right to change the rules of the game, I have the right to order drinks and appetizers."

"Rules of the game? Now I know you're demented. I have no idea what you are talking about."

Megan leaned back in her chair and studied Harry. She really didn't have a clue. And, while she'd seen him angry before, she'd never seen him like this. His anger wasn't a scary anger, and whatever underlined it seemed somehow justified. But she hadn't done anything. She'd kept quiet all meeting and let him shine. He'd done an excellent job.

"You did an excellent job today," she said, trying to return the conversation to safer footing.

His blond eyebrows arched in obvious disbelief. "Excellent? We made hardly any progress. We're nowhere near where we should be at this point."

"Jill's presentation was great. Brett told me he was very impressed."

"Brett?"

"Brett Althoff. He's Evie's grandson and a junior partner in Smith and Bethesda." She saw Harry scowl. "He's sitting in on everything as an unofficial observer, although you know he's the real one responsible for telling his grandfather everything. I know you know that."

"I do." It had just slipped his mind, that was all. He'd been so angry that she'd been quiet during the meetings that he'd forgotten about who Brett Althoff was. Harry had done his research. They were similar creatures, he and Brett. Both were grandsons of self-made millionaires. Both had playboy reputations, although in Harry's case he really didn't think he deserved the moniker. After what he'd seen of Brett today, the man did.

Of course ladder-climbing, man-eater Megan wouldn't hesitate to hedge her bets either. She hadn't looked too unhappy about the attention Brett had showered on her, focusing on him instead of her job.

"Your scotch." The waitress reappeared, setting Harry's drink in front of him.

"Thanks." He took a long sip. The fire burning its

way down his throat did nothing to tamp the tumultuousness raging through him.

"Are you okay?" Megan's words brought him back to reality, to the table.

"I'm fine," Harry replied. He took another long sip before setting the tumbler down. He inhaled to calm himself. "Speaking of Brett, do you think you could have focused a little more on the Jacobsen team today?"

"What?" Megan's hand trembled as she placed the wineglass on the table. "I did my job today, Harry."

"No. If today is the way you work, perhaps you should look for employment elsewhere."

Megan's mouth dropped open. He couldn't focus on her lips. He shook his head, more to clear his head than to emphasize his point. "You didn't do your job today, Megan. You said yes, no and smiled appropriately. Jacobsen pays you to think, to share ideas. Did you do that today? I don't think so. Instead you kept quiet. You didn't share ideas, you whispered God knows what with Brett all afternoon. Compared to yesterday, the dynamic in the room was altogether different, and it was your lack of contributions that made it that way. You let the team down, Megan. You let Jacobsen Enterprises down. You let me down. I'm not happy with you."

And with that the waitress interrupted them again to bring them their appetizer and take their meal orders.

Although she knew she was too upset from Harry's tirade to eat, Megan ordered a stuffed chicken breast anyway. If nothing else, she could pick at the wild rice. Harry thought she'd let the team down. Hadn't he seen how good he was today? She drained the rest of her wine and within minutes another full glass magically reappeared. She drank more of the liquid courage. She knew she'd need it.

"Eat," Harry commanded, waving a homemade, flaky dipping cracker. He popped a bite of the creamy spinach and artichoke mixture into his mouth. "It's delicious."

Megan leaned forward, taking a cracker and scooping some of the dip onto it. Melted cheese dangled, and she used her finger to loop it over the cracker. She hadn't tried this appetizer the night before, and tentatively she took a bite. "It is good."

They ate the rest of the appetizer in silence, Megan knowing that Harry was only biding his time before he launched on the attack again. She decided to beat him to it. They'd fought before—this one she would control.

"So, Harry, you said I single-handedly changed the dynamic in the room. You said you're not happy. Why don't you give me specifics?"

"You want specifics? You would. You didn't pull your weight today. By the end of today I wanted to be beyond pie charts and onto specific terms of the offer. I wanted to see lines of the contract. We should have buried Odyssey Holdings and gotten Evie's in the proverbial bag. None of that happened. We're off schedule."

"It's not all my fault."

"Yes, it is." Harry's gaze bore into hers and Megan flushed.

Forget control. He was right. It was her fault, and she knew it. She'd kept quiet. She'd formed that ridiculous plan to stay away from Harry. Her plan had worked so well that here they were having dinner together. "I'll speak up more tomorrow," she told him.

His sour expression didn't change. "You'll do more than that. You'll concentrate less on Brett Althoff and more on getting Evie's signed on. You'll speak up. You'll voice opinions. That's what you're being paid for."

Megan ignored the rest of his tirade. Harry sounded jealous, but there was no way that could be the case. No man had ever found her that interesting. "I am not concentrating on Brett Althoff."

Harry pursed his lips, disapproval obvious. "Sure looked like that to everyone else, the way you two were whispering together. Don't you know the man is a snake, a playboy? Maybe you like them that way."

It was one insult too many and she reacted without thinking. "If I did like them that way, that means I would like you."

Eyes widening in disbelief that she'd actually spoken the words, Megan's hand immediately covered her mouth. "I'm sorry, that was uncalled for, I mean—"

Harry held up a hand. "Just stop." He reached for his scotch and took a long sip before continuing.

"Since we're being so brutally honest, let's get down to it. You've never made any bones about your feelings for me. I know that you hate me. I'd just appreciate your not making it public any more than you already have."

"Me? Hate you?"

Harry leaned back in the chair and folded his hands across his chest. His expression dubious, he said, "Oh don't play innocent, Megan. Give me more credit than that. I mean, come on. You've spared no expense when you knew you could humiliate me. I just thought that yesterday we'd moved past it."

They had moved past it, until she panicked. Harry Sanders made her more than just simply nervous. He brought emotions to the surface, emotions that scared her. Megan hadn't been raised with happily-ever-after. "What about you hating me?"

"I don't hate you. Your behavior just makes me dislike you immensely, especially when it's at my expense. Could we call a truce? If not, both of our jobs are going to be on the line. I've got to send Grandpa Joe a status report tonight. Can we be partners? Can we put aside our differences and work together?"

Could they? They'd have to. If not, her job was on the line and her income was what kept her mother in medical treatment. Because the IRS did, Jacobsen Enterprises even let Megan claim her mother as a dependent on health insurance. Still, the copays of the medications were outrageously high. Megan had to keep her job no matter what, even if it meant being

partners with the devil in the persona of Harry
Sanders.

"We can do that." A strange feeling came over
her. Partners with Harry Sanders. She'd never been
partners with anyone aside from group members doing a school project. Even in business, even being on
a team still meant working individually. Partners. Just
the word meant being joined, being committed. She
tried to lighten the moment. "So if we don't hate each
other, do we dislike each other then?"

"We could work on tolerating each other," Harry
offered with a grin. When he turned on the charm,
oh! The switch was instantaneous. No wonder women
adored him.

Megan grabbed her wineglass as Harry picked up
the scotch the waitress had unobtrusively set on the
table. His Jacobsen blue eyes twinkled. "Hell, if we
stop sniping at each other we may find out in the end
that we actually can stand each other. Maybe we'll
even be friends."

Friends. A small thrill shot through her. Friends
with Harry Sanders. She liked the sound of that. It
sounded good, safe. They would be friends. Partners.
Snippets of an old 1980's song suddenly flowed into
her head. She didn't remember the exact words, but
the tune was there in her head. The words were something about being friends and lovers.

Lovers with Harry! The waitress put a steaming
bowl of New England clam chowder in front of Megan. Had she ordered that too? It didn't matter. Grateful for the diversion, she lifted the spoon to her lips

and blew gently, not noticing that Harry's eyes had darkened.

"Good?" he asked. His voice had turned husky again.

"Everything's great," she replied without looking at him, for even though he meant her soup, she'd somehow figure out how to make her life the same way—good.

"It's my cousin Claire's recipe," Harry continued, oblivious to her internal dilemma as he made small talk. "She's the manager of Henrietta's, and she also graduated from the CIA."

"CIA?" Megan did look up at that. What was a member of the CIA doing in a five-star, five-diamond restaurant?

His engaging smile told her he was pulling her leg. Harry teasing her? The concept was new and Megan found herself liking it. It made her feel warm. Fuzzy, to coin the cliché. Or maybe she'd just had too much wine. Usually she only had one glass, if that.

"The Culinary Institute of America," Harry clarified for Megan's benefit. "She also has an MBA from Washington University. My family always jokes that Claire gets her way with Grandpa Joe because she knows how to fill up his stomach with good food."

"Then she's probably very successful. The soup's delicious."

As was the rest of her meal. Now that she'd made peace of some sort with Harry, Megan discovered that she'd regained her appetite. The stuffed chicken breast she'd ordered had been cooked to perfection and practically melted in her mouth.

Even better, though, was that she and Harry had seemed to find some common ground. Of course, after their truce there had been an awkward conversation start, with Harry asking her something about her favorite movie.

"Why do you want to know?" Old habits dying hard, she'd instantly retorted, realizing too late from the expression on his face that he'd just wanted to make conversation. She'd hastily backtracked, salvaged her mistake, and they'd gotten into an energetic discussion on the best actors and actresses of all time.

Megan had liked Cary Grant and Jimmy Stewart, while Harry had argued for more contemporaries such as Harrison Ford and Clint Eastwood. They also both liked Tom Cruise.

"What's the world's greatest invention?" Harry asked suddenly.

When she saw Harry's wicked grin, Megan took a sip of her wine. He'd been giving her that look ever since she'd polished off a rich chocolate torte. "Don't even think you'll stump me on that question," she said, buying herself some time.

"Well?" Harry said, leaning back. He had a coffee drink in front of him mixed with Bailey's Irish Cream. "Come on, Megan, you can do it."

"You can't get the best of me." She took another sip of wine. She didn't drink coffee and this was her last glass of the evening, whatever number it was. Three? That sounded about right. The candle on the table flickered, giving Megan the answer she needed. "I've got it! The best invention is electricity."

"Hmm," Harry said as if contemplating her idea. He leaned back again, the movement emphasizing his wide shoulders.

The cad was going to argue her point as he had been doing all evening. Megan beat him to it. "Oh no, you don't! You have to admit I won this one. Our whole style of life runs on electricity."

He arched his blond eyebrows at her. "But isn't electricity just out there? Wouldn't the invention be how to harness it?"

Megan leaned forward. "I don't know. I hated science. That's why I was a business major. But you have to admit I'm right!"

He pretended to be in deep thought. "I guess I'll give it to you."

"You better!"

"Another drink, sir?" Megan practically jumped as the waitress appeared.

Harry also looked startled. "Oh, no thanks. We'd better be going. Just bring us the check."

"Yes, sir," the waitress said, passing the check over.

"We should go," Harry said, his poise recovered. He glanced at the bill.

Megan hid her disappointment. Just when the night had actually gotten fun. "What time is it?"

"A little after ten," Harry said.

"It is late," Megan said, realizing dinner had been over a three-hour affair. She'd been having such fun—with Harry of all people, who would have thought—that she'd lost track of time. "We do have that meeting at eight."

"I've still got to e-mail Grandpa Joe the status reports," Harry said as he handed the waitress the company gold card. "And if I'm right, my sister will have e-mailed me wanting to know why I haven't already e-mailed her."

"Will you see her while you're in town?"

"If I want to live," Harry said. He signed the receipt the waitress brought, stood and came around to help Megan with her chair. His hand cupped her elbow and he assisted her to her feet. A wanton heat coursed through her. "Darci can be a bit formidable."

"I don't even know what it's like to have a sibling," Megan said as Harry hailed a cab. "My mother got sick after she had me. Her disease just wasn't diagnosed properly for several years, which allowed all sorts of damage to occur."

"What does she have?"

"Multiple sclerosis. MS for short."

"Isn't that the disease that attacks the central nervous system?"

"Yes. In her case, she has MS lesions on her spinal cord. Those affect mostly her legs. Anyway, the disease onset came in her late twenties and so I'm her only child."

"I guess the bright side to not having brothers or sisters is that having a sibling can be difficult. Darci and I aren't necessarily that close. We were always competing too much to really become friends. Now that she's married and out of Jacobsen, we've been able to find some common ground. We actually talk more via e-mail that we ever did in our lives.''

''That's good that you're becoming closer.''

''Yeah, I should at least be close to my sister. It's in the rule book somewhere, I'm sure.''

They'd reached their hotel. Again the fire sizzled when their bodies touched when Harry helped her from the cab. Megan's step wasn't quite steady after that, and Harry kept ahold of her as they walked through the lobby and to the elevators.

''I had a little too much wine,'' Megan said, trying to cover her reaction to Harry's touch.

''Understandably,'' Harry said. ''It was a rough beginning.''

''But it turned out well,'' Megan said. They stepped into the elevator and with his free hand Harry pressed the button for their floor.

''I think so too.'' He pressed the door-close button.

''Oh! Wait for me.'' The elevator door retracted as a woman stepped in. She appeared flustered. ''Thanks. I hate forgetting things. I'm already late enough as it is. I left my… Oh! My floor!''

The woman pressed her button and the elevator jolted slightly as it received the command. The woman prodded the door-open button and the minute the door opened she rushed off.

So engrossed in the woman's quick arrival and departure, Megan didn't even realize what had happened. Somehow she'd fallen straight into Harry Sander's arms.

COULD ANYTHING ELSE have felt so right, so good? If he'd known holding Megan MacGregor would be this heavenly, he'd have done it months ago.

She fit him perfectly. At five-eight wearing heels, her breasts crushed into his chest. Her legs molded and intertwined with his. And her lips! Those sirens were scant inches away from being tasted.

They'd called to him to be kissed all night. She'd sipped her wine, her lips surrounding the crystal like a lover. She'd blown her soup cool, her mouth puckering as if she were blowing him kisses. She'd bitten her chicken, and Harry had wished he'd been the fork being sandwiched between those lips. She'd savored that chocolate torte cake, not even realizing she'd closed her eyes as she'd rolled the flavorful bite over her tongue. Would she look that rapturous when he kissed her?

Her brown eyes didn't seem frightened or shocked as he held her in his arms. Her eyes had instead grown slumberous, satiny, sexy. He could read her body's subconscious signals. He knew too many wayforward women, but he knew that right now Megan was not one of them. She put them and their seductions to shame. He had to taste. Just one little taste. He leaned his head forward, lowered.

A ding told him they'd reached their floor. He drew back—the moment denied.

"We're here," he said, reality crashing in, probably for the best. She'd had way too much wine, at least three big glasses. He'd had a few drinks himself, more than his usual. Contrary to what the media portrayed his playboy reputation to be, he never did drink much. He'd had enough of a bad experience in college to prove that it wasn't worth it.

But kissing her! How he wanted to. And she'd been willing. Her left hand dug in her purse for her passkey. He noticed she didn't wear an engagement ring.

He sobered quickly. In this day and age many engaged women didn't wear their rings. He'd learned that lesson once the hard way, when the woman had finally told him she was married.

Yes, it was best they had stopped before it began. Megan was engaged. To a man twenty years older at that. Even if it was simply a marriage of convenience, for that's what it had to be, Harry rationalized, he wasn't about to poach another man's woman. That was something he didn't do, never would do. The one exception had been the married woman he hadn't known was married. He'd broken it off with her the minute he'd found out. She'd wanted to continue the relationship, only wanting a twenty-two-year-old boy to toy with.

So, as much as he might desire Megan, he couldn't act on it. Time to get away. "I need to do those e-mails, so I'll leave you here and say good-night. I'll see you in the morning," Harry said.

Disappointment etched Megan's features, and Harry had to give her credit, she covered it quickly. She slid the passkey into the door to her bedroom. "Good night then," she said without looking at him. He waited until she'd disappeared before he bypassed

the living area of the suite and entered his own bedroom from the hall.

He needed a shower, the colder the better.

MEGAN TOSSED HER purse and her briefcase on the
bed. Harry Sanders had almost kissed her! She knew
it as clearly as if it had happened. His lips had been
less than an inch from hers. If the elevator hadn't
arrived at their floor… She touched her fingers to her
lips. What a night.

She had misjudged him. They'd had fun. Maybe
they could be friends. They could even be love…

No, they couldn't. She had to stop the fantasy right
now, right before she did something stupid like kiss
Harry in an elevator. He was her business mentor, and
that didn't include indoctrinating her into the ways of
womanhood. She'd had that, if her experience even
counted, in the back of Ralph Conner's car. She'd
been sixteen, and her sweet-sixteen kiss had turned
into a makeout session complete with fumbling fingers and lack of inflation on Ralph's part. He, of
course, had blamed her for his poor performance.

Humiliated, Megan had simply sworn off having
sex until she was ready. Unfortunately, with finishing
high school, her undergraduate degree and her MBA,
and taking care of her mother, her experiences with
men had been few, far between and not very satis-
fying.

But Harry would know what to do. With his reputation he'd definitely be more than fumbling fingers.
And the fire that burned in her every time they

touched, she doubted she'd ever be cold where he was concerned.

Even now she still wanted him to kiss her. To divert herself from that thought, she pulled out her laptop and plugged it into the ports on the wall. Within moments she'd checked her work e-mail and taken care of a few business matters.

She then wrote an e-mail to her mother. The last e-mail she needed to do was respond to the one Joe Jacobsen had sent her asking how everything was going. Knowing Harry was sending a status report, she worded her response carefully. "Going well," she typed. "Harry is doing an excellent job with the presentations. Thanks for choosing him to be my mentor. We have finally found some common ground. He'll send you a status report on everything, but if you have questions, don't hesitate to contact me. Megan."

GRANDPA JOE READ his e-mail with interest. Normally he went to bed before ten on a Tuesday night because he had a 6:00 a.m. tee time on Wednesdays. Tonight, though, he'd stayed up late just because he'd known both Harry and Megan would be responding.

Megan had thanked him for making Harry her mentor and said that she and Harry had found common ground. Harry had given a full status report, including that they should have the Evie's commitment by tomorrow. He'd also sung Megan's praises for her idea to market Grandpa Joe. He'd ended saying he'd promised Darci he'd meet her for dinner tomorrow night, and that he'd give her Grandpa Joe's love.

He was such a good matchmaker. Grandpa Joe hummed to himself as he typed his last e-mail of the night.

Jacobsen Enterprises Internal E-Mail
From: Joe Jacobsen *grandpajoe@jacobsen.com*
To: Andrew Sanders *asanders@jacobsen.com*
Subject: Harry

Am forwarding you two e-mails. Read between the lines. He and Megan are definitely getting along now. Start getting ready to weep, and you can thank me later for picking you out such a delightful daughter-in-law.

Chapter Five

"I really think you've nailed this."

"You think?" Megan turned to Brett Althoff. Like the day before, he was still seated to her left.

"Absolutely." He grinned, but his smile didn't affect her quite the way Harry's did. He continued speaking. "In fact, while your team discusses a few practicalities with our legal department, I'm going to go call my grandfather now. If you'll excuse me."

"I'd be happy to." Megan watched Brett give his regards and leave the room. From across the table Harry gave her a quizzical look. Without being too obvious, she sent him a thumbs-up.

He smiled, and unlike Brett's, Harry's smile made her knees weaken. Thank goodness she was sitting down.

As if sensing why Brett left, one of the Smith and Bethesda legal team said, "Shall we discuss the specifics? We have a question on the specific wording of line six on page 15...."

And from there, the Jacobsen guru of law, Jill Benedict's mentor, took charge and led the team through the finer points of the contract.

Four hours later Megan was all smiles. Not only had the Jacobsen team made up the lost ground from the day before, but Brett had returned confirming the fact that Evie's would be sold to Jacobsen Enterprises for the agreed price and terms.

They'd done it. When she and Harry worked together they were an unstoppable partnership.

"You say he's your mentor?" Brett asked her at one point.

"Yes," Megan had replied, a sense of pride filling her. Harry had been a wizard today, and never had she been more impressed. If Joe Jacobsen had been able to see his grandson in action, Megan knew he would have been proud. They'd nailed the Evie's sale based on family values, and Harry had done his family name justice.

"Well, that's a wrap for today," Brett announced. "I think we only have a few minor points to address tomorrow. Shall we give ourselves a bit of a respite and meet at 10:00 a.m.?"

"That sounds fine," Harry agreed. "Jacobsen team meet at the suite at nine."

As they had the day before, everyone began to file out of the room. Brett turned to Megan. "Good night."

"I'll see you tomorrow."

"I'm looking forward to it." He flashed her a smile before leaving. As she closed her briefcase, Megan looked across the table at Harry. They were the only ones left in the room.

"Better today?" she asked.

"One hundred percent," he replied.

A rare boldness filled her. "We should do dinner more often since it worked such wonders."

He snapped his briefcase closed. "We will," he said, "but not tonight. My sister e-mailed me and demanded I go see her. I'm headed there now. In rush-hour traffic, it'll take a cab some time to get to their Central Park West apartment."

"Oh." Disappointment filled her and Megan mentally began to chastise herself. Stupid, stupid, stupid. What had she been thinking, even joking about doing dinner with Harry? She really needed to have more common sense.

"But you shouldn't stay in on my account. If you hurry you can catch up with everyone. They're going to some restaurant down in the Meatpacking District."

"I think I'll do that." Megan grabbed her briefcase and fled, catching up with everyone at the elevator.

"Great job in there," Jill said. "You were awesome."

"Thanks," Megan said as they stepped inside the express elevator that would take them to the lobby. "None of you were too shabby either. Where are you headed?"

"This trendy restaurant that's all the rave," Jill said. "It was even in *Condé Nast Traveler*. Why don't you join us?"

Even though she'd be a fifth wheel to their party of four, the offer sounded tempting. That's just what she needed, to get out. To go do something trendy. To hang with the in-crowd. But then, that wasn't really her. Megan never had hung out with any crowd. She'd always kept to herself. Her mother was her best friend. New experiences were few and far between. She was a chicken, just like her reflection had told her two nights before.

Megan yawned and covered her open mouth with her left hand. "You know, I think I'm still jet-lagged or something. Why don't you four go without me. I think I'll catch a room-service meal and a movie. Besides, I want to call my mom and see how she's doing."

"If you're sure," Jill said.

Megan stepped back a foot. "I'm sure," she said. She parted company with them in front of the building, and hailed a cab back to the hotel.

The suite was quiet and Megan turned on the big-screen television to a music channel. She should not be disappointed that Harry was having dinner with his sister. He'd just told her the night before that he and his sister were trying to get closer, to build their relationship. Having no siblings, Megan didn't understand sibling rivalry at all.

And she had no claim over Harry Sanders. She should not be having crazy, lustful thoughts about him. He was out of her league, out of her sphere. All they would ever be was business colleagues. No matter how cute the fantasy, or how erotic the dream she'd had last night, she was the plain mousy girl from the poor side of town. Men like Harry did not notice, much less marry, girls like her. They needed sophisticated women, women who were naturally glamorous. Megan was none of those things and never would be. She'd learned how to be happy with who she was, had learned to live in her own skin.

But it rankled her a little bit as she ordered an expensive dinner from room service. Complete with a bottle of white wine, Megan had ordered an artichoke soup appetizer, a chicken breast dish with an exotic French name, and since the kitchen had a chocolate layer cake, she'd indulged in a slice of that.

She tried to convince herself she was having the time of her life as she sipped the Riesling, reviewed some documents, and watched an old Tom Cruise movie.

"SO TELL ME ABOUT this woman you're mentoring, Megan," Darci said. She waved her dessert spoon before digging into her parfait. Darci's blue eyes twinkled.

Harry set his spoon down. Dessert had been delicious. "What's to say? She's not quite what I thought she was."

Darci arched her blond eyebrows. "Like how?"

Harry thought for a moment. "Before this trip I would have sworn she had an ax to grind, especially where I was concerned. She did nothing but try to humiliate me in every meeting we'd ever be in together. It wasn't very pleasant. I have to admit, she succeeded once or twice."

Darci leaned back slightly. "Interesting. Yet Grandpa Joe picked you to be her mentor."

Harry lifted his cup of coffee but paused before taking a sip. "That's the strange thing. I really resented it when Grandpa Joe foisted her on me. He sucker punched me into being her mentor during a meeting when he announced it publicly that I'd agreed to mentor her."

Darci nodded, and took another bite of her parfait before continuing. "That sounds like something he'd do. He made me play tour guide for Cameron for a week. Remember that, honey?"

"That's when we started to really get to know each other," Cameron said. New York City's former most eligible bachelor leaned over and gave his wife a kiss on the cheek. Harry looked away. He didn't need to witness the gooey stuff.

"So, you were saying that he tricked you into mentoring her," Darci said.

Harry set his coffee cup down. "Exactly. We had some rough moments at the beginning, but when we finally declared a truce and began working together instead of against each other, the Evie's acquisition just started to click. She's the one that came up with the idea to sell Grandpa Joe. I already told you about that."

The ringlets of Darci's long blond hair bounced just below her chin as she spoke. "She sounds like she's pretty phenomenal."

Harry nodded. "She's definitely an idea person. She sees things from an angle that most people miss. She's the whole reason we were able to get Odyssey Holdings out of the picture."

"You sound like you like her."

Uh-oh. He could tell where this conversation was now leading. "Of course I do," Harry said, adding quickly, "as a business colleague, of course."

Cameron chuckled, his short laugh revealing his obvious disbelief. "If you're sure that's all it is."

"I'm sure," Harry said, deliberately disregarding the fact that he'd almost kissed Megan in the elevator the night before. He may want her physically, but hey, he was male. Wasn't it ingrained to want the female species? Of course it was.

The fact that Megan was somehow different, more of a temptation than any other woman before her had been, was absolutely irrelevant to the equation.

"You know, you don't sound so sure," Darci said. She saw Harry's sour expression. "Oh, don't give me that look, dear brother. I know you. I watched all the girls parade through the house before you moved to your condo in Clayton. You're as red-blooded male as they come. You seem a little more, oh what's the word, animated, where Megan is concerned."

So much for a quiet evening at his sister's.

"She's a business colleague, nothing more," Harry insisted. "I'm still trying to get accustomed to the fact that we aren't at each other's throats."

"We were at each other's throats," Cameron said. He placed his hand over Darci's. "Look at us."

"Perfectly matched," Darci said. "We each draw out the best, and don't get me wrong, occasionally the worst, in each other. But that's what love's about, what makes the journey interesting and worth it."

"Stop it, you two. Now you both sound like Grandpa Joe, and Darci, I remember you complaining about what you referred to as his inappropriate meddling."

"Yes, but he saw what we didn't. He knew Cameron and I were perfectly matched, and he knew we just needed to spend time together to figure it out. Sure, we fought a lot in the beginning, but that's only because each of us was so afraid of being in love. But being in love is wonderful. It would do you a lot of good, Harry."

He'd heard the same lecture from his mother just about a month ago. Now Darci was giving it to him. He needed to set the record straight, and now. "Megan is not my perfect match. Anyway, she belongs to someone else. She's engaged."

Darci's face fell a little but she didn't miss a beat. "Engaged is not married."

"I do not poach," Harry reminded her.

"But if she wasn't engaged, would you be interested?"

Harry gazed at his sister. Now happily married, she wanted everyone to share the joy she felt. "Stop matchmaking, Darci. I'm not interested in Megan except as a business colleague."

Liar, his subconscious shouted. He ignored the little voices shouting in his head. He didn't like what they were saying. While he may want Megan, he knew lust. He needed to keep himself in check, for he knew that lust for Megan was all it was.

"Well, if you aren't interested, then if I were you I'd watch your back," Darci said. She placed her hand over her husband's. "If I know our dear Grandpa Joe, and the matchmaker he is, then I'd say he's pegged Megan as the one for you."

"I think I can handle Grandpa Joe and his meddling matchmaking."

Darci's dubious look told him how much confidence she had in his bold assertion. Actually, he wasn't too confident. After all, he had tried to kiss Megan. "If you're absolutely, positively sure," Darci said.

"I'm sure," Harry said, suddenly ready to escape. Cameron's fingers were tickling Darci's forearm and she'd slapped his hand away. It was too much togetherness, too much joy for him to witness. He hated the mushy stuff.

"Did they ever fill my Jacobsen spot?" Darci asked suddenly.

"No," Harry said. "I doubt Grandpa Joe will. You know how he is. Heck, I don't even know if I'll be named a vice president at all."

"You really should be," Darci said. "I guess what you've always maintained is right. Maybe he is partial to the granddaughters."

"Exactly. I'm not making this up," Harry said.

"Well, if it gets too bad, you can always move to

New York and work for O'Brien. You'd find him a spot, wouldn't you, honey?''

"I found you one," Cameron told her. He ran his forefinger down the tip of her nose.

Definitely time to get going. Harry stood. "I've got to go."

Darci blinked. "So soon?"

"It's eleven."

"I didn't realize it was getting that late. I've got that 7:00 a.m. meeting tomorrow." She stood. "I'm glad you came by, Harry. Let's not be strangers."

She walked him to the door and gave him a hug. "Seriously, don't you dare be a stranger."

"I won't," Harry promised, knowing as soon as he said the words how true they were. "You've got a great guy, Darci. Go keep him happy."

She shot him a lascivious grin. "Oh, I plan on it, believe me."

Harry had a smile on his face the whole way back to the hotel. It had been good to see Darci. He and his sister had actually found common ground.

In fact, maybe that would be the side benefit of this trip, common ground. He'd found it with Darci; he'd found it with Megan. As he slid the passkey in his hotel room door, he wondered if she'd gone out with the team. He tossed his briefcase on the bed and frowned. Was that…music?

Curious, he slowly opened the door separating his room from the living area of the suite. The music seemed louder, and Harry could tell it blared from a music channel on the big-screen TV. A movement to his right caught his attention as a willowy figure dressed in white came back in from the terrace.

Oh my God. Megan was dancing.

Harry's feet froze to the floor. She hadn't noticed him. Instead, she concentrated on dancing to the Latin beat. Her arms above her head, she slowly gyrated her hips in time with the sensual groove. Harry's mouth went dry at the sight.

She was wearing her pajamas.

Never before had he seen a halter top and silk boxer shorts look so good. Not even a Victoria's Secret model could do justice to the outfit the way Megan was.

She continued dancing, one hand now on her hip. The woman was a natural, and despite knowing he was a Peeping Tom, Harry stayed rooted to the spot. He couldn't have moved if his life depended on it. The sight of Megan dancing called him in a primal way that he'd never experienced before.

Like Pan and his flute, Harry wanted to heed her subconscious call, to enter the room, to take her into his arms and clasp her body to his. They'd groove slowly, pelvis to pelvis, breast to chest, every muscle in their bodies intertwined with the rhythm of the song.

A lump formed in his throat as the number turned slower. Megan ran a hand over her throat and across her collarbone before thrusting her arm out again in a gesture bordering on erotic. Harry's feet acted on their own volition, taking a step forward as if an invisible string moved them against his will.

He wanted her. It was that simple. Business colleague be damned. He had to have her. He knew it was a fact of life, just as the sun rose in the east and set in the west.

He took another step forward, and then stopped. There was an almost empty wine bottle on the coffee table. She'd drank just about the entire thing.

He inhaled a deep, calming breath. He could control his behavior. He wasn't a horny teenager any longer. He was a man in control of his body and his desires. She was probably drunk. What she needed right now was to go to bed—alone—because they had meetings tomorrow. She danced out onto the terrace again and he slipped back into his bedroom. Grabbing his passkey from where he'd tossed it on the desk, he exited his room and went out into the hallway.

He hoped she wouldn't be too embarrassed about being caught dancing—in her lingerie no less. His actions were for her own good. He put the key into the door and when the light flashed green, he turned the handle.

IN HER HAZY STATE of dancing, drink and undress, it took Megan a moment to register that the door handle had turned, and that someone was entering the living area of the suite.

She froze. Tom Cruise hadn't been interrupted when he'd danced around in his underwear. But she had. Discovered and cornered, she attacked. ''You're back early,'' she accused.

Unable to help himself, Harry stared. Up close, Megan was even more of a siren, even more of an un-suspecting seductress. The pink fabric barely covering her breasts glistened, and as he approached her he knew his plan had gone horribly awry. He'd expected her—wanted her—to flee to her bedroom. Instead she had planted herself like a deer in headlights. His voice croaked as he tried to salvage the situation. "We have that early meeting," he said.

"That's true," Megan said. She cocked her head to one side and stared at him. Did he look a little flustered? Amazing how free she felt with a lot of liquid courage. "But it's still early and I'm not tired. There's wine left. Do you want some?"

Finding her feet, she moved over to the bottle and poured herself a glass. While she may be caught wearing silk lingerie, not see-through or anything like that, mind you, she was not going to act as if she cared that Harry had seen her next to naked. She had to play this cool.

Her eyes widened as Harry came to stand beside her. He took the glass from her hand and set it back on the table. She bit her lip to keep from swooning. Even with just the briefest of touches, an electric shock had zinged through her. Touch me again, she thought. Even just a whisper of a touch…

"You don't need any more wine," Harry said. "You're done for the night."

Her chin came up, her defiance obvious. Those were not the right words to say. She planted her hands firmly on her hips as a slow song came on, her chal-lenge of his authority obvious. "And you think you know what I need? Do you have any idea, Harry? Do you know what I need?''

He had no clue what she needed, but at that moment, his last resistance shattering, Harry Sanders knew what he needed. He had to have her in his arms. The classic number playing in the background was one of his all-time favorites, and the combination of music, lingerie and Megan was irresistible. ''Dance with me,'' he said. Without waiting for her answer, he pulled her into his arms.

Softness and silk—his brain registered those as his hand splayed across her lower back. The way her lithe body pressed against his was a combination of heaven and hell. Her bare legs intertwined with his.

She fit him as if made for him since before the beginning of time, and it tortured him to know that this was it—this was all he could have.

Her nipples hardened against his chest, and he felt the allure of her lower belly as she closed the last gap between their bodies. His physical reaction to her touch was immediate. He slid a finger under her left spaghetti strap and he caressed her shoulder. It was as silky as the thin material covering her. He lowered her into an erotic dip, the silky pink fabric stretching as her back arched. The boxer shorts rubbed against his maleness. His breath caught in his throat.

Heaven help him, because not being able to make love to Megan would be hell. He wanted this woman with every fiber of his being.

As Harry's arousal pressed against Megan, a fire she'd never experienced spread through her. The sexual sensation was wild, freeing, intoxicating, and she had to have more. As Harry lifted her back out of the dip, she arched her head back, swaying slightly away again before returning to press her chest back against his. He slid his fingers down her inner arm, gathering her closer and letting the music take him further into the moment.

Heaven. She had to be in heaven.

Maybe it was the wine. Maybe it was the music. Maybe it was the dance or perhaps just a predetermined fate, just the climax of all the business and personal tension she'd been under.

Harry Sanders did know what she needed. She needed him. Who cared if she would hate herself in the morning. Right now was about her, about getting what she needed, what she wanted, the irrefutable destiny she had to confirm.

He'd be an excellent kisser, and it was time for her to finally experience that fact for herself. Her body pressed against his, she had to have it all, she had to have Harry's lips.

She moved her hands up, threading her fingers into Harry's hair. The locks were silken strands and he groaned slightly, an almost inaudible sound that thrilled the part of her that was most woman.

It was time to know. Time for the next level. After all, what could it hurt? Just one little taste…that was all she needed.

She brought his head down toward her and kissed him.

His lips were pure magic, and the pleasure that

punched through her from just the briefest touch was overpowering. She stepped back slightly just as Harry's head shot back up. His Jacobsen blue eyes weren't angry, more like shocked, yet still curious.

The moment fled and embarrassment filled her. Having never really seduced a man, she didn't even know how to kiss. She covered with a bad joke. "Oops."

She giggled, her laugh sounding fake even to her own ears. "I guess you can fire me now. Despite our truce, I know you've always wanted to. What I just did is sexual harassment."

To her surprise Harry didn't let her go. Instead his eyes darkened to almost deep blue pools. His grip on her waist tightened, and she felt the power that coiled within him. His arousal still pressed against her stomach.

"I've never wanted to fire you," he said. A flame burned wherever their bodies touched. "And it's only sexual harassment if it's unwanted. And your kiss? That's very, very wanted."

And that being said, he swept his lips back down upon hers.

Megan's Catholic upbringing suddenly popped into her head. She'd been wrong before. Before, dancing with Harry, that had only been purgatory, the place halfway to heaven. Now this, this kiss, this had to be heaven.

Heat hotter than a Colorado wildfire overtook her as his lips pressed against hers, the sensation almost impossible to describe. He teased, he licked, and with a kittenish cry she gave in and opened herself to him. He plundered her mouth then, sending his tongue in to chart new territory. Her knees buckled, but he held her upright, held her tighter against him.

She hated coffee, yet he tasted of it, and Megan had never known any taste sweeter and more nourishing. Bolded by the desire sweeping through her, she licked his lips with her tongue, the texture sending more heat pooling between her legs. She wanted more, she wanted his mouth, she wanted to mate her tongue with his, and when her mouth plundered his, he let her have whatever she wanted.

Bells rang in her head.

"Phone," Harry said, and then suddenly he was pulling away, crossing the room. As if he was in a haze, she watched him pick up the receiver. "Harry Sanders. Oh, hi, Darci. Yeah, I got back safely. I didn't know you wanted me to call. I thought you'd be busy with Cameron."

His sister. The phone call acted like a sobering shower, washing away all the magic of the music and the wine. She'd been standing in a suite making out with Harry Sanders. She'd been kissing him like there was no tomorrow, and if Darci hadn't called…

Megan didn't want to think about how wanton she'd been, or what she may have done had the phone call not interrupted. Kissing Harry…oh! No matter how good the kiss they shared had been, she knew she was going to hate herself enough for that in the morning. Even worse, already her head was starting to hurt from drinking too much alcohol. She'd had more wine in two days than she usually did in two months.

Megan began backing away. She needed to get to safety before he finished the conversation. She turned and without worrying what he thought of her, she walked away as fast as she could without losing the rest of her dignity. Fleeing to her room, she shut the door behind her with a decisive click.

The magical dance was over.

HARRY SET THE PHONE down and stared at Megan's closed door. He touched a finger to his lips. Had the kiss really even been real? He raked a hand through his hair, trying to clear the thoughts jumbling for position. He already could predict the future and he didn't like it. Tomorrow Megan would mumble something about the kiss being a mistake and they'd go on their merry way with a terrible tension hanging between them.

He mentally cursed himself. He was an idiot and worse. He'd just committed the sin. He'd poached another man's woman. He'd stuck his tongue halfway down her throat, pressed his arousal up against her silk-clad body so she could feel every bit of his desire, his need. Harry poured the rest of the wine down the bar sink. To top it off, Megan hadn't even been sober. She'd been tipsy, and taking advantage of her the way he had made him a cad, a heel of the lowest order.

He'd not only let her down, but he'd also let himself down. He'd sworn to himself that never again would he be with another man's woman. And tonight

.he had. He'd kissed Megan. He'd been intimate with the woman his grandfather wanted him to mentor in business matters, not in sexual ones.

Torment filled him. Couldn't someone else share the blame? Damn Darci and her ill-timed phone call. She'd interrupted the best kiss of his life. He could tell that Megan had little experience, none of the practiced art of many of the women he'd previously kissed. But that hadn't mattered. She had natural seductiveness, a natural passion that had sparked something deep inside him, something no other woman had ever come close to touching.

Damn Megan for being engaged, for working at Jacobsen. Why couldn't he have found her somewhere else, working for another company?

Why? Did that horrible question ever have an answer? Or as usual, was fate mocking him, this being simply another example.

He pounded his fist onto the table, not hard enough to do any damage, but hard enough to vent the pent-up frustration he felt. He couldn't blame anyone else. It wasn't Darci's fault. She'd saved him from making a mistake. It wasn't even Megan's fault. She wasn't the man-eater he'd originally thought she was. It was all his fault. He knew better.

He had to stay away from Megan MacGregor. He couldn't bear to be around her, to see her and remember the most phenomenal kiss of his life and know that that was it, all it would ever be.

He'd tell Grandpa Joe to find her another mentor as soon as he returned to Saint Louis. An e-mail wouldn't do it, this was something he'd have to admit to his grandfather face-to-face. He wasn't looking forward to having the meeting, admitting that once again he'd failed to meet his grandfather's expectations. But it was better than the alternative, seeing Megan every day and knowing that no matter what, he couldn't have her.

He headed into his bedroom. He had to purge her from his system. The question was going to be how.

Chapter Six

"It was a mistake. I'd been drinking wine and I—"

When Megan had begun her spiel earlier that morning, Harry had put up his hand, and Megan had stopped speaking. "No excuses," he had told her. "Let's just put the incident behind us and move forward, okay?"

That cute little wrinkle had formed between her eyebrows and the mouth he had kissed just last night had puckered into a little O. He knew she hadn't expected his brusque manner, and part of him regretted using it.

"Okay," she had finally said before going to take her seat next to the man whom Harry had dubbed a few hours ago as the now very annoying Brett Althoff.

The very man who, if he'd move any closer to Megan, would be sitting in her lap. Harry frowned. Time to get this show on the road so they could all go home. Cutting out at 3:00 p.m. sounded ideal, especially if it meant getting Brett away from Megan. Tomorrow could just be a casual Friday. Maybe both teams would have everything finished by noon.

"My grandfather, Joe Jacobsen, is prepared to be in New York Monday morning for the contract signing," Harry announced. His gaze caught Brett's. "As lead counsel for this sale, do you agree that we've reached that point?"

"Absolutely," Brett replied. He turned to look at Megan and said, "Your Megan has been a fantastic negotiator, and Evie's is ready to sign. We'll type up the documents and review them tomorrow."

"Good," Harry said. He didn't like how Brett was now whispering something to Megan. She blushed. Harry gritted his teeth. "Shall we meet at ten?"

"Ten," Brett agreed without diverting his attention from Megan.

"Then I guess we're done here," Harry said, dismissing everyone. They began to file out. However, usually the first one out of the room, this time Brett hadn't budged. Instead he and Megan were talking.

A raw and rare jealousy filled Harry and he clenched his right fist to his side to regain his control.

His anger was with himself.

How had he let her under his skin? He'd broken his vow never to poach. Now, from the looks of it, Megan had already moved on.

Thankfully there were only two more business days, with two weekend days in between, to go. Then, when he returned Monday he would be free from the torture that was being around Megan.

Last night had been terrible. He'd been unable to

achieve deep sleep, the vision and texture of Megan's kiss tormenting him and not letting him rest. Harry had woken up several times in a sweat, his body aroused and ready and wanting her. He'd given up on sleep and taken a long cold shower at 5:00 a.m., but the hard cold spray of water hadn't erased the memory of the touch of her lips, the feel of her skin under his fingers.

Magic interrupted. Those were the words to describe last night. Megan suddenly laughed at something Brett said, and raw bitterness filled Harry. He couldn't keep doing this to himself. He couldn't keep wanting her, wanting what he couldn't have. He had to purge her from his system.

But how? He'd mulled that question over and over. Usually he would just sleep with the woman. As soon as she wasn't a challenge, as soon as he'd sampled the wares so to speak, he usually found himself unimpressed, bored, and definitely ready to move on. While the encounter was mutually pleasurable, Harry knew it made him cold-blooded. It made him a playboy. It made him the whole lot of nasty things that people, especially the women, called him when it was all over.

And he knew he deserved every one of the labels in the past, every one of the insults hurled at him.

For it was his fault that he'd broken their hearts. There had been nothing wrong with the women, his heart just hadn't been in the relationships. He couldn't sustain interest after the challenge abated. He'd catch

them, and after that the thrill was gone. His cousin
Shane was the same way.

But Harry wanted to change. Maybe it was simply
aging, turning thirty. He'd done so much better the
past year, really curbing his playboy attitude and actions, really trying for a long-term relationship.

But the women he'd dated, he just hadn't been able
to love them.

Thus he'd failed each time, once again disappoint-
ing Grandpa Joe in another aspect. His grandfather
wanted to see Harry married so that his grandmother
would have great-grandchildren.

But none of his retrospect solved the current problem of Megan. Maybe he should just sleep with her.
Get her out of his system. She'd been willing last
night; he knew women well enough to know. Just
because it went against all his vows…

Do it! the devil on his shoulder whispered, adding
things about how soft and silky she'd been. How
much of a dynamite kisser she was. How she was
under his skin. And after all, he was a playboy with
the reputation of a love-and-leave-'em snake. She'd
surely not be surprised.

And as for his vow, could a leopard really change
its spots? His conscience wrestled with that. And for
the sake of argument and his subconscious, maybe her
engagement wasn't serious. Maybe the office gossip
was wrong. After all, he was discovering that Megan
wasn't quite the immoral career-ladder climber that
he first thought she was. Her kiss last night had almost

an innocence to it, and Megan didn't have the capacity to lie very well.

Which brought him back to the fact that maybe he shouldn't sleep with her to purge her from his system. He shouldn't take advantage of her to solve his problems. He was thirty, after all, and he could be a man in this situation. Perhaps they could be friends.

Friends. That had a nice safe ring to it. He'd never had a woman friend before; he'd slept with all of them. But being friends with Megan, well, he was much more mature now. He could do it.

Maybe he should just take her to dinner to prove it to himself and her. It could solve all their problems until they returned to Saint Louis.

If she was his friend he'd stop seeing her as a challenge. If he put her in the box marked Friend, then she could be that, and that was all she would be. After all, he was a grown man. Dinner should be safe. He'd ask her as soon as that annoying Brett Althoff left the room.

MEGAN GLANCED UP. Her forehead creased slightly. Why was Harry still shuffling papers? The meeting was over. Shouldn't he be leaving? She looked up and caught his intense blue-eyed gaze. Even the dark blue rims surrounding the edges of his eyes had darkened.

Uh-oh. She'd hoped he wouldn't wait for her, but it was obvious he wasn't leaving until she was ready.

And she wasn't leaving, at least not with him.

She turned back to Brett. ''I need to talk to my

boss for a few minutes. Shall I meet you in the lobby in fifteen minutes?''

"I'll see you there." He stood and left.

Megan looked back at Harry. "I assume since you're still here that you wish to see me?"

"I do," Harry said. "I thought since we both agreed to put last night's incident behind us that we could go to dinner and figure out a way to stay friends. I don't want things to get awkward between us."

He'd asked her to dinner. He wanted to be friends. At the beginning of the week Megan would have killed for an offer like that. Friends with Harry. That was so much better than being adversaries.

But now, after last night, there was no way she could simply just be *friends* with Harry Sanders.

She'd kissed him. Perhaps it hadn't meant anything to him, but if the phone hadn't interrupted she would have been begging him to make love to her. After her lack of control, her wantonness, she couldn't be Harry's friend. Because of her out-of-control behavior, her deep desires, she had to stay away from him completely. She couldn't indulge even a little bit, for where Harry was concerned, Megan knew she couldn't drink in moderation.

Not that she'd ever been an alcoholic, but for a short time, when she had been seven, her mother had been a slave to the bottle. Her mother had finally gone to Alcoholics Anonymous meetings and sobered up. Her mother hadn't touched alcohol since.

Now, where Harry was concerned, Megan had to

be the same way. She had to stay away from him. It would be too easy to fall off the wagon, to fall back under his easy charm.

She'd always want him, but early in life she'd learned that one didn't get what she wanted. If one did, then Megan would have had a normal childhood and a healthy, normal mother.

She'd learned to accept her fate and not let it depress her. At least she had a mother who loved her. Some people didn't even have that.

So Megan had become one who made lemonade when given lemons. Then she somehow sold that lemonade for a fantastic business profit. That's who she was, a survivor and an eternal optimist. She'd been doing it all of her life.

But Harry…unfortunately Harry Sanders wasn't a lemon. Far from it. No, he was chocolate cake. She'd eat every last bite, and when it was all gone, that would be it. To complete the metaphor, she'd have ruined her figure for a few moments of fleeting gratification.

Maybe it was wise that she'd made other plans, even though she knew he wouldn't like them.

"Dinner sounds nice but I can't go," she told Harry.

Harry appeared thunderstruck. He leaned toward her. "What?" He clicked his briefcase closed.

He wasn't going to make this easy, was he? "I can't go to dinner with you," she repeated, forcing the words out.

He jerked a hand through those silky blond locks

she'd fisted only last night. Fighting the urge to touch, she clenched her fists.

"You can go to dinner with me, Megan," he said. "Stop avoiding me. You aren't a coward. It's only dinner."

She slowly turned her head from side to side, dreading what was about to come. Maybe she'd been misguided. "No, I really can't go with you. I told Brett I'd have dinner with him."

"You what!"

Megan winced. She deserved hearing that tone of his voice and seeing the stricken expression on his face. She knew he wasn't going to be happy. "He asked me to dinner. I accepted."

"The man is a playboy."

"So are you," Megan retorted. She covered her face with her hand. "I'm sorry."

Harry ignored her. A muscle in his cheek twitched. "Business or personal?" he asked.

Megan jutted her chin forward. *I'm so sorry, Harry, but it's better this way.* "Personal."

Harry's face darkened and the muscle in his cheek ticked more. She knew he held his anger in tight check. "I see. You'd ruin months of negotiations and business dealings for a fling with the great Brett Althoff."

She knew she had to keep firm, hold to her resolve. She needed space away from Harry, and she intended to do nothing with Brett. "It's not a fling, it's simply dinner. Just like we would have had." Oh that sounded lame.

He didn't buy it. His face contorted as if she'd slapped him. He suddenly gave a short laugh, the movement changing his angry features into a cold, harsh neutral expression. The movement chilled her.

"Always looking for the better catch, aren't you, Megan? Aren't you satisfied with one? How does he trust you anyway? I thought you were different. I can't believe I was so stupid. Well, I won't be blinded again." And with those words Harry walked to the open conference-room door.

Megan suddenly gripped the conference table, glad for its support. Thankfully, no one lurked in the hallway. No one else ever needed to know about this conversation. Suddenly, Harry turned around. His stare was so intense his eyes didn't blink as his gaze locked onto hers.

"Have fun on your date, Megan. Do yourself a favor, though. You better be really sure of Brett and his intentions. If you do anything, and I do mean anything, to derail this acquisition, you better hope he'll hire you. Because if you blow this deal and it falls apart, I'll make sure you're out of Jacobsen Enterprises so fast that your head spins."

And with that he left her, leaving the door wide open. Megan bit her lower lip to hold back the tears. She'd known it wasn't going to be easy to stay away from Harry, right? But she was strong. She could handle breaking even the beginnings of friendship with Harry so that she never fell out of control again.

Megan's hand still trembled as she put the last of her papers in her briefcase and went to meet Brett.

HARRY PUNCHED THE down button, glad to see that the elevator doors opened within seconds. He punched the button for the lobby and the door-close button. Chivalry be damned. Megan could just wait for the next one.

So much for making a noble attempt at being friends. She'd already dismissed him and moved on to the next fish to fry. Every time he questioned her reputation, she'd do something to reconfirm it. And to think she'd had him fooled the other day. Had he not had to have a conversation about focusing more on the merger than on Brett? He had, the night after she'd been so quiet during the meetings.

Brett Althoff was lingering in the atrium lobby when Harry stepped out of the elevator. "Is Megan coming?" he asked.

Harry schooled his features and voice into neutral. "She's on her way down now."

"Good." Brett paced a moment, and Harry paused, sensing that Brett had more to say. "You're lucky to have her on your team," Brett said.

"I know," Harry said. He took a step toward the door, making his impatience to go obvious but yet not rude.

Brett wasn't to be dissuaded. He grinned and continued. "Oh, come on, Harry, you and I are the same type. Surely you've hit on her. Man to man, what's it take?"

Only nerves of steel, of having had to many a time deal with the full force of Grandpa Joe Jacobsen, kept Harry from plowing his fist through Brett's face. Brett wouldn't have deserved it, though, for Harry knew he was guilty of everything that Brett alluded to.

Because Harry knew he wanted Megan. He'd kissed her. He would have made love to her. Brett's insinuation was like a pot calling a kettle black. Very deserved. Harry clenched his hands at his sides.

"I'm a professional and she is my associate," Harry finally managed to say through gritted teeth. As much as he wanted to defend Megan more, she had made her choice. Still, he added, "There's nothing to tell except that Megan is a special woman. She's not either your type or mine. She's not a player."

"I think she'll play just fine," Brett said with a knowing look. "She's full of fire, that one. Hot underneath those sexy suits she wears."

Harry's stomach rolled. Brett and Harry were about the same age. Was he, Harry, a player like Brett? No, he couldn't be. Please tell him he wasn't, that he had changed. Looking at Brett, and his attitude toward women, especially Megan, sickened Harry. He had to get away from Brett.

"Oh, there she is," Brett said as Megan exited the elevator.

"Enjoy your dinner." Harry strode off and hailed a cab.

"Where to?" The cabdriver asked. Harry blinked. He didn't know. He needed to get out, to go somewhere, to find some warm, willing woman who would make him forget Megan.

But if he did, then he'd be the same as Brett. I've changed, Harry told himself. He would not act in old patterns. He would not handle rejection by escaping or slaking his lust somewhere else. It was time to grow up. "Marriott East Side."

The cab pulled away from the curb, but not before Harry saw Megan and Brett emerge through the revolving doors. Bitterness filled him. If she was going to cheat on her fiancé, why did it have to be with scum like Brett Althoff?

And why was he, Harry, jealous? He couldn't still want Megan after all of her misbehaviors. He'd made a vow never to poach, or get involved with another man's woman. So if Megan was one of those women who was involved, and cheated, then he didn't want her anyway. Right?

The situation had no answer.

The cab pulled up to the hotel. A uniformed doorman was already opening Harry's cab door. Harry strode under the arched colonnades and through the ornate lobby. Maybe a shower would clear his brain, wash Megan from his soul.

Something had to or he was going to go insane.

DINNER SHOULD HAVE been fun. After all, after being her tour guide and showing her the sights, Brett had taken her to one of the ritzier restaurants in Manhattan, a place where the upper-class single businesspeople hung out after a hard day at the office. They hadn't arrived until around eight.

"Isn't this place great?" Brett had said upon their arrival. Megan blinked, her eyes already turning red. If you liked smoke-filled rooms and elbow-to-elbow crowds, this was it. But she'd never been into that scene.

"Great," she lied as the waitress showed them to the table in the middle of the restaurant. Everyone seemed to know Brett and kept stopping by. The men leered at Megan, and the women dismissed her outright.

By dessert, almost two hours later, Megan was ready to go back to the hotel.

"You're sure you don't want dessert?" Brett asked. The waitress leaned over to clear a plate, giving Megan a view down her shirt. Great. No wonder Brett had been so enraptured earlier.

"I'm fine," Megan replied. She'd made a mistake. Staying in the suite, even holed up in her room, would have been better.

"Coffee?" Brett asked.

"No," Megan said. She glanced at her watch. "I really have to get back to the hotel now. I need to call my mother."

The look on his face said it all as Brett took one last swig of his drink. "Your mother?"

"My mother is very ill. I always try to check up on her before she goes to bed."

"What's wrong with her?"

Spoken like a man who really cared. Not. "She has MS," Megan said.

Brett shrugged as if that was of little consequence. Megan guessed he probably didn't even know what the disease was.

"Come on, Megan, you can miss one night. Your

mom will understand. You're in New York City. Live a little. Let me take you to see some more of the sights. There's this club right around the corner, and then I want to show you my apartment. It's got a phenomenal view of the Empire State Building.''

Probably from his bedroom, Megan thought, and she certainly wasn't interested in that. She wasn't interested in him at all.

She'd definitely made a mistake. She'd thought she could kill two birds with one stone—get out of the hotel and be away from Harry and perhaps learn some business tips from Brett.

But Brett wasn't interested in business. He'd been overly demonstrative all night. Worse, all his flaccid touch had done was make her miss Harry's. Harry's fingers had been firm and strong whenever they'd made contact with her skin. Harry's touches had sent shivers of desire quaking through her, not shivers of revulsion.

In fact, the men couldn't be more polar opposites. Harry might have the reputation as a playboy, but Megan had never seen him act as anything but a pure, perfect gentleman.

Brett, on the other hand, disgusted her. He was a player through and through, a womanizer of the first degree. She chided herself for her foolish decision. She never should have agreed to go to dinner with him. She'd only done so to get away from Harry, to give herself a reason not to sit in her hotel room all night.

She'd made the wrong choice. Sitting in her hotel room, while lame, at least had self-respect.

"I really need to get back," Megan said to Brett. She made her voice firmer this time. "It's been a lovely dinner."

"You can't just leave me." Brett appeared shocked. Did women never reject him?

Of course not, Megan thought. He was rich. Look at all the examples of predatory females who had stopped by the table tonight to say hello. There had been at least a half dozen.

But she wasn't one of those females. All dinner with Brett had proved was that there were worse things than being alone.

"I've got to go. It would probably be better if we just say good-night here. You certainly don't have to accompany me in the cab to my hotel."

"The night is young." Brett made another attempt to woo Megan as he tossed a large wad of bills down on the table.

Megan faked a smile and stood. Did the man never quit? "Yes, but for me it's old. You've been a charming dinner companion and I've enjoyed tonight."

Well, that was a huge white lie. The lie worked, though, for seeing she was serious about leaving, Brett stood and grabbed his Armani jacket. "You're sure I can't convince you to see the view from my apartment? It's like all those romantic movies."

"No." If he was waiting for her to say "Maybe another time," he was going to be disappointed. She pushed a loose strand of brown hair behind her ear and began walking to the exit. Brett followed.

Never a cab around when you need one, and they needed two, a fact she made clear to the doorman. "It'll be a moment," the doorman assured her.

"Thanks," Megan said. The May night was warm, but still she shivered. Brett had moved into her space.

"You are going to let me kiss you good-night," he said.

No way. Megan stepped back. "I don't think that would be wise."

"What?" He clearly wasn't expecting that response.

She grimaced. She'd learned in graduate school how to handle his type—flatter and deny at the same time. "I might not be able to stop," Megan said as she planted a wistful expression on her face.

She made the childish gesture of crossing her fingers behind her back. Forgive me for the lies I'm about to tell. "We've got work still left to do, Brett, and I don't mix business and pleasure. I'm sorry, but kissing you will have to wait." Just where was that cab?

He leaned in, his breath smelling of smoke and the whisky he'd had with dinner. Yuck. So opposite from Harry. "Just one won't hurt," Brett said. He reached for her. "I'll make sure we stop. And if we don't, my apartment is around the corner."

"I can't risk it." A flash of yellow screeched to a halt. *Thank you!* Megan put her hands on Brett's

chest, pushing him back away from her as the doorman opened the door to the cab. ''Good night.''

And within mere seconds Megan was safe, on her
way back to the hotel, her head in her hands for making such a disastrous mistake.

THE SHRILL OF THE PHONE shattered Harry's concentration, or lack of it actually, on the movie showing
on the big-screen TV.

''Megan?''

''No. Why would I be Megan? Isn't she there?''

''Hello, Grandpa Joe.'' Harry glanced at his watch.
It was almost eleven eastern time, which meant it was
almost ten in Saint Louis. Grandpa Joe was being a
night owl.

''So she's out?''

''She went to dinner with a friend,'' Harry replied.
He didn't think Grandpa Joe needed to know that
Megan's friend was the legendary lady-killer Brett
Althoff, and that Megan was just as bad as Brett when
it came to using people.

''Oh,'' Grandpa Joe said. ''Anyway, I called late
because I wanted to catch you.''

''I've been in all night,'' Harry said. He muted the
sound of gunfire coming from the movie on TV.

''Really? That's not like you,'' Grandpa Joe said.
Harry declined to contradict his grandfather. He'd
learned it wasn't worth it.

''Anyway, I'm calling because I wanted to tell you
personally how pleased I am with the way the negotiations concluded,'' Grandpa Joe said. ''Your team

did a good job. I'll be in New York Sunday night so that I'll be there for the media ceremony and press conference Monday morning. I've already got Sally making the arrangements for you and Megan to fly home Monday afternoon. Everyone else leaves Friday, well that's tomorrow afternoon. Are you listening?''

"Uh-huh."

"Anyway, Sally will e-mail the itineraries first thing tomorrow so that everyone can get planes home."

"That sounds fine." Harry blinked. The action-adventure movie wasn't the same without sound, and did Grandpa Joe just say that Megan was staying in New York for the weekend? He hadn't been listening, had he?

"So has Megan done much sight-seeing?"

"I don't know," Harry answered honestly. He had no idea where she'd gone after leaving Smith and Bethesda. Hopefully not Brett's apartment, although it wasn't his business if she did. Unless she screwed up the negotiations… He'd missed something again.

"What did you say?" he asked Grandpa Joe.

"I said you need to take her out. You still aren't listening, are you? I said that you know the city pretty well. I don't want her sitting around the hotel being bored. Take Megan to the museums or something tomorrow after you get everything finalized."

No way. Not after her behavior with Brett. Not when she's engaged. Time for evasive tactics. "She keeps pretty busy," Harry said.

Grandpa Joe didn't buy it. "You are getting along, aren't you?"

"Of course," Harry said, knowing that this was not the time to bring up opting out of being Megan's mentor. "She's just busy, that's all. She's a self-starter."

Grandpa Joe seemed satisfied. "Good. Good. She's a sharp one that girl, and you could do worse. Of course, come to think of it, occasionally you already have."

Trust Grandpa Joe to bring up that. Had Harry ever pleased him? From the way it sounded, the only way Harry might ever please his grandfather was to bring home Megan as a granddaughter-in-law. Like that would ever happen.

"Stop trying to be a matchmaker," he told Grandpa Joe. "She's not my type."

"You wouldn't know your type if it reached up and kissed you on the lips," Grandpa Joe snapped. "Really, Harry, you're a fool."

And the line was suddenly dead.

Harry replaced the receiver. No, being a fool would be letting Megan MacGregor even further into his life. She wasn't his type, and she had reached up and kissed him on the lips.

A clicking noise alerted him to her presence. She was opening the door to her hotel room. The adjoining door from the suite was open, and he saw her enter. He swallowed his pride. He could at least be polite. After all, she was home before eleven. "Hey," he called.

"Hey," Megan replied. He watched as she set her briefcase down. She walked into the living room. "I didn't expect you to be here."

He shrugged. "I'm not the playboy my reputation maintains. I do have evenings in. Quite a few actually. And *Mission Impossible* is on."

"One or two?"

"One."

"Maybe I should have stayed in. I like Tom Cruise," she said.

"I remember," Harry said. He'd memorized every word of their conversation Tuesday night about actors and her favorite movies.

She smiled as if the memory caused both happiness and sorrow. "Well, it's late."

Harry's internal radar went off. Something had gone wrong on her date. He knew it as certain as he breathed. "You can stay and watch the movie. I promise not to bite or fight."

Her eyes widened and he saw how weary she was. Obviously not a good night. Her next words and the way she said them confirmed his intuition. "Only if you won't ask me how my date was."

Part of him inwardly danced with glee. It had been horrible. But now was not the time to gloat. Now was the time to support Megan, whether she deserved it or not. "I promise I won't ask. You can tell me if and when you want to."

It was as if the floodgates opened. Megan clenched her fists and waved them for a minute. "It was terrible. You were right. He's an absolute playboy jerk from hell and I couldn't leave fast enough.''

Woo-hoo! Harry checked his glee. Still, he gave her a grin and tried to cheer her up. "Was the food at least good?"

"I wish," Megan said with a resigned shrug of her shoulders. She sat down on the opposite side of the sofa and Harry immediately wanted to draw her into his arms and give her a hug. Only the sudden thought of the mythical fiancé kept him from acting on his urges.

"And the place was smoky. I need a shower. I stink like cigarettes. I hate that," Megan said. "It was awful, Harry, awful."

Distaste filled her features. She was so opposite of the cold-blooded woman who'd started out the evening. Which woman was real? Did it even matter? Not really.

The truth hit him in the face. He still wanted her more than any other woman he'd ever met.

Megan drove him so crazy that he wanted to break every vow, every promise he'd ever made to himself. Perhaps in the future he would. But not tonight.

Tonight Megan needed to know that not all men were like Brett Althoff, and that Harry Sanders was not a playboy. Sudden inspiration hit him.

"Why don't you go get a shower and join me? The movie just started. In fact, if I remember, you've already seen it, so you won't really be missing anything."

The offer made sense, and suddenly Megan didn't

want to go directly to sleep. She needed Harry to understand; she needed…to be back on even footing with him.

Oh, who was she fooling? She wanted him. She kept running away, but every path she'd taken had led right back to Harry. Every plan she'd made regarding Harry had backfired. Life had been so messed up, how could a movie hurt?

She stood. "Thanks for the offer. I'll take you up on it. Just give me a few minutes."

His husky voice called her back before she stepped through the doorway to her bedroom. "You're safe with me, you know."

She looked at him, her breath lodging somewhere in her throat. Unlike Brett, Harry didn't scare her.

At least not in the scary, petrified sense. But whereas Megan may be "safe" with him, she knew she really wasn't. He made her feel things she shouldn't feel—desire, longing, need. And there Harry lounged on the sofa, every inch pure male. The temptation was too great.

A moth to a flame. The combination of Harry, a sofa and a Tom Cruise action movie was insurmountable. But Harry, he was the key ingredient.

She escaped to her room, but she could contemplate nothing but the evening ahead as she showered, the hot water beating down on her skin. Would he kiss her again? Was he even thinking about it the way she was? She touched her fingers to her lips and then, shaking her head to clear it, turned off the water and toweled dry.

Stepping into her bedroom, she debated for a moment wearing her silk loungewear. No, that would be inappropriate. While she may want him, they were business colleagues. As much as she wanted him to kiss her, after his nasty comments at the end of the meeting, silk would send the wrong message. She definitely didn't want Harry to think she was going from Brett to him. She finally dressed in sweatpants and an oversize T-shirt. She went out into the living area.

He arched a blond eyebrow at her. "Not as sexy as the other night, but probably a better choice."

She'd been right. "You think?"

"Yeah," Harry said. "Come sit down. If you're up to it, I'll give you a backrub to make up for my nasty comments earlier today about firing you."

How could she refuse that? She was a sucker for backrubs. She often gave them to her mother, but with her mother's fingers not functioning normally, Megan never got them in return.

A backrub was like winning the lottery. Following the gesture of Harry's hand, Megan sat on the sofa where he'd indicated. Warm, strong fingers found the tension in Megan's shoulders and he began to knead it away.

Megan's head dropped to her chest as Harry's fingers worked their absolute magic. Tom Cruise could wait.

It must have been at least ten minutes before Harry spoke. "I do want to say I'm sorry for the way I threatened you this evening. It was out of line."

He'd apologized. She rolled her neck, allowing him

better access. His fingers danced over her skin, soothing and relaxing. "It's okay, Harry. I shouldn't have said yes to a date with Brett."

His breath was close to her ear. "But I shouldn't have been unprofessional. I let my emotions rule."

"You've done a good job on leading the team. I was wrong to jeopardize it. I know better." She began to drift off. She was so tired and his fingers felt so good. She let herself go.

"It's not a good situation to ever be in, even if it is just business," Harry continued. "I know I'm certainly not as trustworthy where women are concerned. Maybe that makes me a skeptic, a tried-and-true cynic. He must be very special."

What was he talking about? Harry kept mentioning some he. Did Harry think she was dating someone? She thought about opening her mouth to ask him, but that would require movement. Effort. Right now she couldn't even open her eyes if she wanted to, not when a sense of deep contentment filled her instead as the last of the bottled-up tension and stress drained away.

She leaned back, her head falling against the sofa. She could get used to this. Harry giving her backrubs. Harry apologizing. Just Harry being Harry.

Did he know how much she'd come to like him? Even respect him? He was such a special man. She should tell him. Those thoughts also drifted away.

"So much for a movie," she heard Harry whisper. It sounded so far away. She felt herself lifted up and carried. Heavenly. Were those covers coming to her chin?

Warm lips gently pressed her forehead. "Good night, sweetheart."

What a wonderful dream. Harry tucking her in and kissing her. Mmm. She rolled over and fell deeper into sleep.

HARRY WATCHED MEGAN sleep for a few minutes. She looked angelic. Although her dark hair wasn't long, it still framed her face. He resisted the urge to smooth out some loose strands. Kissing her on the forehead—meant as purely platonic—had been guilty pleasure enough.

He'd meant to relax her with a backrub. While he hadn't meant for her to fall asleep, he was actually glad she had. She'd wake up in the morning, and once her initial shock and embarrassment of being tucked into bed was over, she'd see him in a whole new light. He hadn't made a move. He hadn't taken advantage of her.

It had taken all of his mettle to remain focused only on meeting Megan's needs. With his hands massaging her neck and shoulders, the heat between them had been almost unbearable. He had definitely wanted to kiss her, to taste her soft skin, to feel her beautiful body next to his.

But he had tamped his own desires down. Convincing Megan he was an honorable man, not a playboy like Brett, was so much more important than what

Harry needed physically. Friends, he told himself. They would be friends. He'd see to it.

And, if he guessed correctly, hopefully by tomorrow she'd see him a little differently, this time for the better, making that friendship possible. That made the ice cold shower he now needed well worth it.

He hummed to himself as he clicked the lights off throughout the suite and headed for the bathroom.

Chapter Seven

"Good morning."

Harry glanced up as Megan stepped into the living area of the suite. He let his gaze run over her. As always, she was radiant. "Good morning to you," he replied. He gestured toward the bar. "Fresh coffee and bagels are over there."

"Thanks." As she crossed the expanse, Harry took a moment to study her. Could he find out why she was such a siren to him?

There was a simply a basic grace to Megan that called him. The blue pumps she wore added to her height, lengthening her legs. Her new wardrobe, today a pale yellow fitted sheath dress with matching jacket, accented her dark hair that was pulled away from her face with two in-style barrettes.

She set her briefcase down by the bar and helped herself to a cup of hot chocolate and a bagel.

"Are the others coming?" she asked.

He'd been so upset at seeing Megan and Brett together yesterday that scheduling the meeting had slipped his mind. "You know, I forgot to mention it yesterday," Harry said. "But being creatures of habit, I'm betting everyone will assume that like yesterday and the day before we'll meet here before we go over."

Megan took a bite of her bagel and Harry watched her lips move. She had such perfect, kissable lips. He blinked. He didn't need those thoughts dancing around his head right now.

She still hadn't approached the table where he sat, so he gestured to an empty chair. "You can join me. I don't bite."

She smiled at that, and balancing her plate and hot chocolate, approached him and took the chair to his immediate left. "I know. You told me last night I'd be safe."

"And you were."

"I was," Megan confirmed. She seemed nervous. Harry's internal radar went on full alert. Something wasn't quite right. "Thank you for that," she said.

"You're welcome. We have to work together. We might as well get used to that."

He saw the hesitation on her face before he heard it in her voice. "Speaking of, I was thinking that, given our circumstances, we may want to approach your grandfather together and ask him to assign us to different people for the duration of the Stars program."

Only yesterday he'd been thinking the same thing, but now, hearing it from Megan's own beautiful mouth, Harry suddenly couldn't conceive losing her.

He did what any good businessman did in an unforeseen crisis, he hedged.

"Are you certain?" he asked. "We've been under some pretty intense strain this trip. Perhaps once we return to the office it will be better."

She smiled wistfully, as if she wished that were possible. "Harry, we both know the situation won't change. We're either fighting or I'm doing irrational things like kissing you. Behavior like this isn't in either of our best interests."

He knew she was right, but he couldn't admit it. He opened his mouth to say something, anything, but at that moment the rest of the Jacobsen team showed up. Harry exhaled. Perfect timing. He now had most of the day to decide what to do, what response to give Megan.

After a brief meeting, the team headed over to the Smith and Bethesda offices.

As soon as Megan stepped out of the elevator she sensed that something was wrong. Harry must have felt it too, for immediately he slowed his pace and fell into step beside her as they walked into the conference room.

"Are you okay?" he asked.

"Is it my imagination or is everyone staring at me and then looking away?"

Harry glanced around the room. She heard his hiss of angry breath. "It's not your imagination," he said.

"Great," Megan said. What an idiot she'd been. She should have fought her fear and stayed with Harry in the hotel suite last night. Instead she'd gone to dinner with Brett Althoff, a man who had obviously said something about her, done something to her. She knew it as certain as day. But what? And how to deal with it?

"I'll deal with Brett," Harry said as if reading her thoughts.

She couldn't let Harry champion her. She made her mess, she'd get out of it. "I fight my own battles," Megan said. She jutted her chin forward, staring down a female member of the other team who had dared to stare a bit too long.

"Not this time," Harry said. He gestured to a seat next to the one he'd sat in for all the meetings. "Sit here today."

"Harry, I am not going—"

"You are. It's an order. As leader of the team I'm going to deal with this," he said, and Megan, seeing the determined expression on his face, did the logical thing. She sat down in the chair, that once Harry sat, would be to Harry's right. She watched him stride off, approaching Brett like a knight going into battle.

A sudden relief filled her. Harry would deal with the situation. She'd always fought her own battles, but just this once… It was a good feeling. She trusted Harry. He'd take care of her.

HARRY WASN'T A lip-reader, but as he walked up to Brett, his intuition told him exactly what Althoff was saying to the group of men standing around him. He knew from the sly glances, the lewd looks, the leers in Megan's direction.

In days gone by he himself had been in the center of that circle of attention. How often had he regaled the guys with tales of his latest conquest? Seeing Megan's stricken face, he mentally apologized to all those women, even those who had been players and who had known the score going in.

It didn't make what he'd done right. And even if Megan did cheat on her fiancé, that didn't mean that she didn't need someone coming to her assistance in this matter. For playboys needed to become gentlemen at some point, and Harry knew it was now time to teach that lesson to Brett, even if the man didn't understand it right away.

"Hot," Brett was saying as Harry approached. "A wildfire. I couldn't believe it. Who would have guessed under those suits she wears? She definitely can mix business and pleasure."

Harry checked his immediate distaste. Teaching Brett a lesson didn't involve public humiliation unless absolutely necessary. "Ahem," Harry said as he joined Brett's inner circle. "Good morning."

"Harry," Brett said with a jovial grin. "Ready to get this final show on the road?"

Harry inclined his chin slightly, his return smile not quite reaching his eyes. "In a moment, Brett. Would it be possible for us to have a personal word?"

Brett didn't look too concerned. He shrugged. "Sure. Outside in the hall okay?"

"Perfect," Harry replied, following Brett from the conference room. The two found a quiet spot in a small corridor where they wouldn't be overheard.

Brett faced Harry. "So what's up?"

Harry took a deep breath. Time to begin. "Brett, I'd really appreciate it if you would stop spreading falsehoods about Megan, a member of my team."

As Harry emphasized the word *my*, Brett's face fell. Then he smiled again as if it was all a good joke. "Falsehoods? Please, Harry. I don't know what you're talking about."

"Let me spell it out for you. I told you last night that Megan wasn't a player. She's not in your league and is not accustomed to your typical behavior. Thus, you need to stop playing your game of telling your associates—" Harry stressed the word to emphasize the word *associates* so that it meant cronies "—a bunch of improper comments about Megan. Your words can be construed as sexual harassment against a member of my team."

"Oh please." Brett shrugged. "We had a great time on our date. Everyone asked me about it. There's no harm in telling people about having a great time."

Harry stared at Brett. "I'd have to disagree with you. There is a problem when it's embellished. She told me otherwise about having a good evening. As a member of my team, she's not to be trifled with."

Brett leered suddenly and gave a short laugh. "Oh, I get it. You have a thing for her, don't you?"

Harry kept his temper in tight check. The truth of his feelings for Megan, or his motivations, was not available for public consumption, or relevant here. "Trying to shift the guilt of your inappropriate actions won't work with me, Brett. Weren't you raised to be a gentleman? Gentlemen do not tell their business associates that their date was a wildfire, especially when said date left early. Lying is never appropriate.''

''How old are you? You sound like my grandfather,'' Brett said. ''I have a reputation to maintain.''

And therein, Harry saw, was the difference between himself and Brett. Harry didn't want the playboy moniker hanging around his neck. Brett still embraced it, courted it. Couldn't see that a woman may not want him. Couldn't see that his behavior was demeaning.

At that moment Harry knew he had changed. Satisfaction that he had done the right thing filled him. He had grown up.

Brett, though, still didn't get it. He shrugged. ''She loved being with me. Do you know how many people stopped by our table during dinner last night? Being seen with me is an honor in this town.''

''She's not from this town and for the sake of harmony during our final contract review today, I'd suggest you cease holding any further conversation that demeans Megan and causes people, especially your associates, to stare at her.'' Steel laced Harry's voice.

Brett didn't look impressed. ''Or you'll do what? We've come too far in these negotiations and you're all leaving Monday. Tell her to get over it. Like anyone would ever believe her. She's a nobody.''

Harry laced his fingers together and managed an outward appearance of calm. He could argue that Megan was a somebody, but that would just give Brett kindling to work with in a counterattack. No, Brett didn't care about Megan as a person.

Therefore it was time to pull out the mythical hammer—the final blow—Harry held behind his back. Grandpa Joe had always taught him not to use the hammer unless absolutely necessary, and in Brett's case, knocking him over the head with it was a necessity.

"Do you know who my brother-in-law is?" Harry asked.

Brett gave a disinterested sneer. "Why should I?"

"Because his name is Cameron O'Brien." Harry watched the recognition cross Brett's face. Cameron O'Brien, CEO of O'Brien Publications, ran one of the largest media empires in the world. "I'm sure he would listen to Megan, and you know how slanted, yet unlibelous, the media can be. Scandal does ruin one, doesn't it? Or perhaps instead you'll find yourself with no press coverage. After all, even though this is New York, the city still has a pretty small A-list, doesn't it? And Cameron and my sister Darci, and Cameron's sister Kit and her husband, they are still the toast of the town if I'm not mistaken?"

Brett paled slightly. He bit his lip and his eyes narrowed. Harry knew he'd hit that nail literally right on the head. Being a playboy and losing those coveted invitations was worse than death. Medieval perhaps, but being shunned in the "right" society still occurred no matter how much old or new money one had.

"Therefore, since you do have a reputation to be

concerned about, I would suggest that regarding Megan, you keep your mouth shut now and forever,'' Harry replied.

Then Harry smiled as he cemented the promise. "If not, if I ever hear of it, I will personally help you shut your mouth one way or another, and yes, Brett, that is a threat I will carry through on."

And with that, Harry turned on his heel and left Brett standing there, his mouth gaping open in absolute disbelief. Harry strolled back into the meeting room and took a seat by Megan.

Brett followed about two minutes later. His hand shook slightly as he gripped his coffee mug. "Shall we begin?" he said.

Harry noticed he didn't look at Megan once. Satisfaction filled him. Brett had too much to risk for the nobody he considered Megan to be. He wouldn't say anything more. The lesson, while it might not ever become crystal clear, had at least been learned.

There was always someone out there in the world who carried a much bigger stick.

Today, it had been Harry.

The rest of the meeting went smoothly, if not overly long, and if anyone had been expecting some kind of show regarding Megan, it didn't occur. Harry had quietly settled everything out in the hallway, a conversation that Harry knew Brett would never repeat.

No man liked being put in his place.

"Thank you," Megan whispered as the meeting wrapped up later than expected, around 3:00 p.m. The other four members of the Jacobsen team had left twenty minutes ago for LaGuardia Airport. "I'm not sure what you did or said to Brett, but it worked."

Harry turned his head to gaze at her. They hadn't sat next to each other at any of the Smith and Bethesda meetings before and he found his face right next to hers now.

He jolted back, surprised at their proximity. His heart warmed. She was so beautiful, so earnest in her gratitude. Fiancé or not, Megan never deserved Brett's treatment. "Don't worry about what I did," Harry said. "That's what friends are for."

"Friends," Megan repeated. "I like the sound of that. So in gratitude can I take my new friend to a casual dinner, you know, as friends?"

She blushed slightly and Harry's throat constricted. She was so beautiful. But he could handle dinner. They could be friends.

"Sounds good," Harry said. "I'll meet you back at the hotel. I've got a few things to finish up here."

"I'll see you there."

Harry watched Megan leave. Brett had left the meeting long ago, and now just a skeletal Smith and Bethesda crew remained to finalize Monday's media event. Harry smiled to himself. He didn't know where he and Megan were going with their volatile relationship, but they had finally turned the proverbial corner.

He turned to finish the last few details. He had a dinner to get to.

WHEN MEGAN RETURNED to the suite, she discovered the message light on the phone was blinking. "You have a package at the front desk,'' the attendant told Megan when she called down. ''I'll have it sent right up.''

Ten minutes later Megan gasped. Brett Althoff had done one thing right. On his tour of the city yesterday, he had regaled her with stories of what was hot and what was not. And right now, in Megan's left hand, she held two tickets to the hottest show on Broadway.

Megan turned over the card accompanying the tickets. ''Good job on negotiations, enjoy. J.J.'' the card read. The tickets were from Joe Jacobsen.

How sweet of Harry's grandfather to reward them and give them something to do now that the rest of the team had gone home to Saint Louis. Well, theater would round out a nice evening with Harry. Friends. Finally. She went to get ready.

Chapter Eight

Harry hummed to himself as he opened the door that led from the hotel hallway directly into his bedroom. Everything for Monday's media event was settled.

He entered his en suite bathroom and fifteen minutes later he'd showered, shaved, and was dressed and ready to go. When he stepped into the living area, he found Megan already waiting for him.

She silenced the TV, the word MUTE appearing in the upper right corner. "Hi," she said. "How'd it go after I left?"

"Everything is set," Harry replied. He strolled in and grabbed a bottle of water from the mini-refrigerator. "We are free until Monday and then we can go home."

As Megan stood up, Harry noticed that her short black skirt fell only to midthigh. Whoa. When had her legs gotten so long? And her breasts, highlighted by the V-neckline and fitted waist of her silk shirt, so full? His libido kicked into overdrive. There was nothing he wanted more right now than to spread her out on his bed and make long slow love to her.

"Where to?" he said instead.

"Broadway," Megan replied. She held up two tickets in her hand. "This show is all the rage."

Broadway? How did she get tickets to the rage of Broadway on such short notice? And on a Friday night. He knew Megan. He hated looking a gift horse in the mouth but intuition told him that something wasn't right. He tried to make his voice casual. "Where did you get those?"

"You hate Broadway? It's not a musical." Her face fell and he hated himself for upsetting her. He placed his bottled water down and reached for the card she held out. Reading it confirmed his fears. Good old meddling Grandpa Joe. Matchmaker from hell.

The conversation that Harry and his grandfather had had came rushing back. Grandpa Joe wanted Harry to date Megan. Wonderful.

No wonder his grandfather had been so insistent that Harry mentor Megan. His grandfather figured that, like Cameron and Darci, throw the Harry and Megan together and love will naturally take over.

Here would be one more area that Harry would disappoint his grandfather in. He and Megan were friends. That was it. He admired her. He respected her, well, he respected everything about her except the fiancé. And he didn't love her.

"Harry, you do like the theater, don't you?" Megan repeated.

Harry glanced at Megan. Megan didn't know any-thing about Grandpa Joe's matchmaking. She wasn't a part of Grandpa Joe's scheme, well, at least not an aware party. And as disappointment etched her face, Harry refused to let his meddling grandfather ruin the evening.

Grandpa Joe would just have to be disappointed. Harry and Megan were only going to be friends.

"I love going to the theater," Harry said. He took the tickets from Megan's hand. "He got us excellent seats. Are you hungry for dinner? We did have a late lunch."

"Not really," Megan said.

"Great. How about we go to the concierge level, have a few appetizers from the buffet and go to dinner after the show?"

"That sounds good," Megan said, her wariness dissipating.

Harry offered her his arm. "Shall we go?"

"Absolutely." She'd brightened considerably and she reached forward and allowed him to loop her arm through his. Even through his suit jacket, he could feel the warmth of her touch. "I'm looking forward to tonight," she said, her voice suddenly shy.

He stopped, resisted the urge to kiss her, and smiled down at her instead. "So am I," he said. "So am I."

AND THE NIGHT was just about everything he'd hoped for, Harry reflected later. She'd loved the play, and now, as their dinner date at the French restaurant be-gan to wind down, she'd mellowed even further.

Perhaps it was the wine, but unlike the dancing Megan of a few evenings ago, this Megan seemed more relaxed, more at ease, more at peace with herself. The result, as far as Harry was concerned, made her even more desirable, more intoxicating. This was a woman who was comfortable in her own skin, who grasped life with both hands.

He admired just about everything about her.

She challenged him, yet he still wanted to be with her when she wasn't a challenge now that they were just going to be friends. She'd never bored him yet. He'd never met anyone like her.

He blinked, catching the fact that she'd been waving her dessert spoon in front of his eyes for a moment.

"Penny for your thoughts, spaceman."

He rested his chin on the back of his hand and smiled at her. "I was thinking that you're different from a lot of women that I know."

She seemed slightly taken back by his honest answer. "That's good, of course," he added quickly. Then he deliberately lightened the moment with a cliché. "You're like a cool breeze on a hot day."

"Flatterer," Megan retorted. Her brown eyes twinkled. "I bet you say that to all the girls."

"I plead the Fifth," Harry said. She grinned at him, her smile causing delightful laugh lines around her mouth. He wanted to trace the alluring creases with his fingertips. What would they be like to touch? If he did, would she turn her head slightly and catch his wayward finger in her lips?

"You know," Megan was saying, diverting him from those dangerous thoughts, "I've been meaning to ask you a question. This may sound weird but don't take it wrong. Could you please explain to me what you mean when you keep referring to me and some other man?"

Oh. Only one way to answer. The truth. "Your fiancé," Harry replied.

Her forehead creased and her lips pursed together. "What fiancé?"

"Your fiancé. The one you're engaged to. The—" he paused, then just rushed forward "—the elderly man who's been seen around the office with you. Your fiancé."

"He's not my fiancé."

"Then who is he?" The words slipped out before Harry could recall them. Heaven help him, he sounded jealous.

"My mother's fiancé."

"Oh." Stunned silence fell over Harry. Megan wasn't engaged. The man was her mother's fiancé. A flicker of joy began to shoot and spread through him. Megan wasn't engaged; he hadn't poached. He hadn't broken his vow.

Relief filled him, to be replaced by immediate want. Down, he told himself. It shouldn't matter. They were just going to be friends. Friends. That was it. Oh, who was he fooling? She was free. Not engaged. Available. And he wanted her with every fiber of his being.

"I guess word at the watercooler had it wrong,"

he managed to say finally, for, after all, Megan was still staring at him as if he was a little bit crazy.

"They did, and that would explain a lot." A whole lot, actually, Megan thought.

No wonder Harry had thought her a woman of loose morals. He had thought she was cheating on a fiancé. The concept, that Megan would even have a fiancé, was almost ludicrous. She was married to her job. She had to make sure her mother got the medical treatment and medications she needed.

Time to explain, to put his mind at ease. "My mother has been engaged to Bill for over a year. He worships the ground she walks on but she refuses to marry him."

It was Harry's turn to look confused. "I don't understand. When you love someone you always want to be with them and—"

Impulsively Megan reached her hand across and covered Harry's. A warmth immediately began flaring between them. "I told you already that my mother has multiple sclerosis. What this means is although she can still walk, she's pretty much confined to a wheelchair because walking tires her out so much. We're just glad she isn't paralyzed, which happens in some cases. Anyway, Bill loves her, but because of what I call her foolish pride, she keeps putting him off until she's well. Hopefully that's going to be soon. She's scheduled for medical treatment in a few weeks. It's a new medication coming onto the market and we're hoping it'll help."

"Tell me about it," Harry said. He laced his fingers

through hers and those beautiful blue eyes radiated sincerity.

"You really don't want...."

It was as if he could read her mind, for none of the men she'd ever been out with really cared or wanted to know about her mother. His gaze intensified. "I do. Seriously. Tell me, Megan. I want to know."

So she told him about how the disease attacked the central nervous system, causing inflammation that when healed left scars. It was these scars that caused the nerve messages to become unable to travel, and thus the body unable to function properly.

"The nerve messages just don't go through. She has a progressive form of the disease and it just gets worse as she ages. We're just grateful she's not paralyzed. That can happen, but so far her medications have helped. They cost us over three hundred dollars a month, and that's just our copay."

Harry listened to every last word, and throughout the whole conversation he held her hand, his thumb gently rubbing the inside of her palm.

By the end of the evening Megan was secure in the knowledge of two things. One was that Harry Sanders was one special man. The second was that, she wanted him with every fiber of her being and her want was not the slightest bit alcohol induced.

She attempted to withdraw her hand but instead Harry stopped her by tightening his grip. He covered their linked hands with his free hand.

The movement of both of his hands surrounding hers shot waves of longing throughout Megan's body.

With every fiber of her being Megan wanted Harry—
wanted to feel more of his touches, wanted his body
pressed up to hers, wanted him joined to her in the
intimate, timeless ritual of becoming one.

And the thought suddenly struck her that maybe
subconsciously she had always wanted him like this,
with this uncontrollable passion. Maybe that's why
they'd never really gotten along before.

Maybe the reason they'd always had such conflicts
was that beneath the conflicts there had always been
an undercurrent, something buried deep that both had
somehow instinctively feared.

That something intangible and untouchable was life
altering, and the unknown in itself was always scary.
Thus Harry and Megan had reacted to their mutual
desire by fighting it and thus fighting each other.

For, after all, Megan thought, what did you do
when you met that person, the person that made life
mean something? That made life matter? That made
you whole?

And what did you do when you weren't sure of his
responses? It was called risking your heart.

At that moment Megan knew the truth. Harry Sanders was that person, the one who was the yin to her
yang. She'd never met a man quite like him, a man
that somehow knew her better than she knew herself,
a man that brought out the best in her.

A man that she was falling in love with each and
every day.

Oh, they could rub each other the wrong way, all
right, but in doing so, they made each other stronger,

better people. And he'd been her defender, her champion, her mentor, her sharpening board. She respected him, desired him, loved him.

His feelings, beyond that of wanting her physically, remained a mystery. But Megan wasn't worried about that. Not now. Tonight she was ready to face her fear.

Tonight she was going to risk it—to take that last necessary step in bridging the gap between her and the man she was falling in love with.

No matter the consequences, tonight she didn't want to run away. Tonight she didn't want to play games with herself, to convince herself that Harry was just some guy she worked with.

Tonight she wanted the kiss and all its promise. She wanted the things that had been denied to her the other night when they'd drawn apart after that earthshattering kiss. She wanted to feel Harry's bare chest next to hers, his strong legs intertwined with hers, his firm body joined with hers.

She couldn't wait any longer. It was time to leave the restaurant.

He must have sensed some change in her emotional state for he signaled the waiter to bring the check. "Megan," Harry said. "Are you ready to leave? I'm sorry, I didn't realize how late it is. It's almost 1:00 a.m."

"Take me to the hotel," she replied, her voice huskier than she'd ever heard it before. His blue eyes widened in surprise and she tightened her fingers on his to emphasize her meaning.

She had to risk rejection. It was now or never, his

answer be darned, and Megan had always been a straight shooter. She made the first move. "No games, Harry. I'll put myself on the line. I want you. A great deal. And now that you know I'm not some woman of ill repute with a stashed fiancé back in Saint Louis.…"

His expression changed, and that encouraged her. "Megan, are you saying…" he began.

She added her last free hand on top of the pile of their other intertwined hands. "Take me to the hotel and make love to me, Harry."

They were words every man wanted to hear, but they were also words of torture to a man trapped by a table and the need to pay the bill. However, Harry's body had already come to full attention with the promise of the night ahead, and he was suddenly grateful the table hid his arousal that pressed against his trousers. He gazed at Megan, and an overwhelming need to touch her face, to stroke her cheek, overtook him.

He'd wanted her for so long. Tonight wouldn't be about slaking lust. Tonight was about them and their newfound relationship. They could be both friends and lovers.

"As soon as we pay," he managed to say. "I…"

Harry fell silent as finally the waiter approached. Harry lifted his hands from Megan's, and breaking contact with her was hell.

Immediately Harry missed her warmth, her fire. He dug into his wallet and before the waiter even handed over the leather folder, Harry handed him a credit card. He waved the man's surprise aside and reached for Megan's hands. It was like a shivering man getting a blanket. Instant warmth and relief filled him as he regained the passionate shelter he needed.

"I want you too," he told Megan. Her mouth formed that cute little O, and how Harry wanted to kiss her right there. More torture. He wouldn't be able to kiss her until they got in the cab.

And then... How he made it out of the restaurant in one piece he wasn't sure. The five minutes it took the waiter to run the credit card and bring back the slip seemed to be five hours. Neither Harry nor Megan spoke, afraid words could break the mood, yet silence saying more and building more passion than any words ever could.

Finally they were in a yellow taxicab headed for the hotel.

"Megan." He said her name and she turned her face toward his. With his right hand he reached out for her, and using two fingers he traced her mouth, her lips silky under his touch. She parted those perfect lips and he traced her top lip once more before changing the position of his hand to run the backs of his fingers across her cheek. Then he flattened his palm, ran his fingers across her left ear before he encircled the base of her neck. Then, and only then, did he gently guide her forward as he lowered his lips to hers.

Sweet merciful heaven. If their first kiss had been earth-shattering, this one rocked the universe to its very core. It was everything a kiss should be—tender, timeless, full of promise of the night to come.

Harry pressed his lips to hers, savoring the known, yet somehow different, sensations shooting through him. Kissing Megan was fresh, new, unlike any other kiss ever. And how she responded, her kisses eager.

Harry drew back, lightening the kiss to just feather touches between their lips. He wanted to taste her mouth and savor its sweetness, but not until they were safe in the privacy of their hotel suite.

It didn't matter what room, but since he had a key to his handy, Harry guided Megan to his bedroom door. The green light flashed its approval, the chrome handle gave, and the door shut behind them with a final click as it locked into place.

Megan was then in his arms, planting intoxicating kisses along his neck. Fire and need consumed him, but in his desirous haze, Harry knew he didn't want to be seen as a playboy rushing a conquest to bed.

This was Megan. He wanted everything to be perfect for her. She was different, special. She was— could it be true?—everything. He wanted their lovemaking to be as beautiful as she was.

"I'm sorry," Harry whispered, which was all he could manage under the circumstances of his throbbing body. He couldn't rush her, and to give her time he said, "My manners. I should offer you something. Are you hungry? Thirsty?"

"Only for you," Megan said, the intensity in her voice shattering his last thread of control. Both of her hands laced up into his hair and she tugged gently on the golden strands, the movement guiding his lips back down to hers. "Kiss me, Harry."

"Oh yes," he murmured and brought his lips to hers. "Oh yes."

Megan's eyelids fluttered closed. This man, this man she'd fallen head over heels in love with, was finally kissing her again.

She'd never have guessed Harry to be a take-it-slow lover. After all, weren't playboys known for quantity? Again she'd been wrong about Harry. That thought, dancing somewhere in the recesses of her mind, pleased her. Heat pooled inside her.

Megan went to deepen the kiss but he darted back slightly. Her tongue, instead of finding the inside of his lips, traced the outline of his bottom lip. His fingertips caressed her chin. "Savor," he whispered before he brought his mouth fully to hers again.

And so savor she did. His kisses were midnight magic. Even after he lowered her gently onto the turned-down bed, he still continued to just kiss her, savoring her mouth and igniting a passion long dormant. Her head fell back onto the soft pillow, the wrapped hard-candy mint some housekeeper had put there skipping to the carpeted floor with an unnoticed plop.

Could he kiss her forever? She discovered not only that he could, but also that he could take her even higher as finally his tongue wet her lips, his sensual way of asking for entrance. She parted her lips, permission granted, and tentatively his tongue touched hers.

The movement of Harry's tongue on hers was soft and gentle, yet steady and seductive. Sensation after dizzying sensation tumbled over and through Megan as Harry explored and ignited fire after fire just from kissing and passionately plundering her mouth. His firm lips found her seeking tongue and tugged gently, the slight suckling making her moan with pleasure.

The man could kiss.

And as those sensations washed over her, he gave her mouth a brief respite as he lowered his lips to kiss her neck and the base of her throat. She'd worn a button-front silk shirt, and she gasped with pleasure as Harry kissed her breast directly through the silken layers of fabric. Her back arched to meet him, and soon the buttons gave way under his moving fingers and the shirt fell aside although not off.

"I love that you wear lace," Harry whispered and his lips tugged at her nipple through her bra before his stroking fingers pushed the lace lower and he covered her bare flesh with his mouth.

Cherished was the word that came to Megan's mind as Harry laved passionate attention on both her breasts. This lovemaking was about her, about treating her as the most special woman in the world.

Harry suddenly gathered Megan into his arms, pulled her up and freed her from the barriers of her clothing.

Within moments she was naked to the waist, his chest was bare, and his mouth was crushing down upon hers with a more forceful, yet still tender, urgency that could no longer be denied.

"You are so beautiful," he whispered against her neck, and his hands and face slid lower, and much later, after he'd lavished massive attention on her breasts again, Megan felt her skirt pushed up as Harry lowered himself even farther.

"More lace," he murmured and Megan gasped and clutched the bedsheet as he lowered his mouth to the lace barrier. Heat pooled through her, her legs already a molten jelly. Deft fingers moved the lace aside and then she felt the direct touch of his lips, and those pleasurable sensations sent her spiraling over the edge.

Here also, Harry worried little about time. He took his time kissing her, sending her spiraling to the brink and back several times before he got around to taking off her skirt and sending her black lace underwear flying.

Not that he stopped his attentions there. He simply lowered his head again and lavished attention differently, using different flicks and strokes of his tongue to send her cresting and peaking once again.

Had it ever been this intense in her life? As Harry gently nipped her inner thigh with his teeth she didn't care about lovemaking intensity or even remaining in control at all.

She cared about nothing right now but making long, slow love with Harry Sanders. And even though they'd not completely joined together, Megan already knew the answer to any lingering doubts. This was the best lovemaking of her life.

His mouth came back to mate with hers again and

as she tasted his passion mixed with hers, she dug her fingers into the hardness of the taut muscles on his back. His skin was a silky-smooth texture under her fingertips, and she stroked it to memorize the feel of it, of him. She ran her hands over his dress pants, cupping his hard buttocks. It was time. She needed all of him. ''Off,'' she said.

Still kissing her, he lifted himself over to the side and he began to work on unfastening his leather belt. The room was dark, but Megan could still see him move in shadow as he stripped completely, his boxer shorts also falling to the floor.

He slid back close to her. As their bodies again touched, Megan felt his naked ˋskin, his hardness pressing against the top of her thigh.

Her hands reached out, touching him, holding his hard flesh and stroking it. This was all just for her. Wetness beaded on the tip and she slid the silkiness over him, eliciting from Harry a wanton groan.

His mouth captured hers again and he made his desire, his own need known. ''I have to get something,'' he said as he began to slide away, but by this time Megan was an unquenchable wildfire.

Her heart flared at his thoughtfulness to protect her, but she wanted him—every last bit of him. The quick conversation ascertaining that both were healthy and that she was on the Pill took mere seconds between passionate, demanding kisses.

And then his hands were again everywhere, stroking, stoking her fire higher, and finally Harry lifted himself over her and gave in to the frantic need that consumed them both.

"Oh my," Megan breathed as Harry fully slid into her. Every nerve ending tensed, every ounce of her body concentrated on the pleasure he gave her with each and every perfect thrust.

She'd never understood that a woman could have internal and external passionate sensations until now, and Harry gave her each one many times as each of his thrusts drove her farther and farther into the world of suspended timelessness.

But not even those sensations prepared her for the climax, that moment when Harry truly joined himself to her by spilling himself inside her. Megan swore she saw heaven as her hands fisted the sheets, her head fell to the side, and her body ceased to be as it spent itself becoming one with his.

Afterward there were no words needed as Harry gathered her into his arms and they rested until need for each other overtook them again. Megan lingered in the joy of it all as they made love again, and once more before, finally, Harry simply held her quietly. He pulled her head to his chest and wrapped his arms around her, his breathing becoming slow and steady.

Although secure in his arms, Megan frowned. Something was out of place. She blinked. Sunlight was flickering in around the edges of the curtains. They'd made love for hours. "It's daylight," she said.

"Mmm-hmm," Harry said as sleep began to fully claim him. He simply ran his hand up into her hair and pulled her head back to his chest. "Sleep, darling. We've got no place we have to be today."

But the oncoming sunrise gave rise to Megan's doubts. She'd just made love with Harry Sanders, many times. What would tomorrow even bring? How would she act? She had feelings for him, feelings she didn't know if he shared. Now that he'd had her, would he even still want her?

A raw panic filled her as her earlier bravado to risk fled. "Harry, we've got to talk. We work together. What will we do when this ends? How will we act? What—"

His finger gently touched her lips, causing her to immediately cease talking. Harry's blue eyes were open and the intensity in his gaze comforted and frightened at the same time. She was comforted by his warmth, and frightened by the unknown future. He continued to trace her lips, and she instantly kissed his fingertip.

"Who says it will end?" he asked.

He gathered her tighter into his arms and she drew courage from his strength. "We've proven we can take things one step at a time. Rest, Megan. Rest assured. Get some sleep, darling."

Megan closed her eyes, mentally pushing away the fright caused by all the current unknown variables. There was one thing she knew for certain.

As the night ebbed away, Megan knew that she irrefutably loved this man who held her tightly in his strong arms.

A thousand thoughts jumbled in her head as he

shifted, drawing her closer as he drifted into sleep. Lemonade from lemons. Harry wasn't a lemon. He was chocolate cake. Could she have her cake and keep him to? Could she… She fell into a dreamless sleep, secure in the fact that at least for now, he held her safely in his arms.

Chapter Nine

Six hours of deep, contented sleep was about all Megan was able to catch. There'd been this tingling feeling of awareness and she'd rolled over, shifted, and found Harry's blue eyes studying her. She could stare into his eyes forever. The inner light blue had darkened to match the outer rims. And the way his eyes twinkled...

"Good morning," was all she managed and then he'd kissed her. From there she'd been lost.

They didn't leave the bed until two. Then, after a long shared shower, they'd hit the town of New York late Saturday afternoon about three-thirty.

Although she'd done some limited sight-seeing with Brett, Megan certainly hadn't seen all of Manhattan. Harry made up for that by taking her over to the United Nations building, down through SoHo, and then to Rockefeller Center.

Glad she'd worn her comfortable shoes and a twin-sweater set, Megan was prepared for the day being in the high sixties.

Harry himself dressed down, but his idea of casual was a polo shirt and chinos. Since they were dressed for the outdoors, they'd placed a to-go order at a small café, caught the subway uptown and eaten lunch in Central Park.

"I wouldn't have pictured you for a subway person," Megan said as they opened their take-out bags.

"Why not? It gets you from point A to point B," Harry said.

And at that moment Megan knew that there was more to this man, this former playboy, than anyone else knew. After lunch he impressed her more, taking her to Strawberry Fields, the area of Central Park set aside in memory of John Lennon.

She knew Harry didn't have much interest in the deceased rock star, but she wanted to go so that she could tell her mother all about it. John Lennon had been her mother's favorite Beatle. Once there, Megan made many mental notes so she could later describe the experience to her mom.

Afterward, as they walked along a pathway, the thought that Harry had done it for Megan had touched her, and her love for him grew even more.

Then she and Harry had holed up on a park bench for a while and, his arm a comfortable weight around her shoulders, they had watched the passersby as the early evening began to settle in.

A rare peace filled her, and there, sitting on the park bench, a vision struck her. She could see herself sitting right here with Harry, fifty years from now, doing exactly the same thing.

The thought sent butterflies soaring throughout her stomach, and Megan shifted slightly. "What's wrong?" Harry asked.

"Nothing," Megan lied, for really, even though yes, there was something wrong, it was nothing she could share with him.

For no matter his earlier words of assurance that their relationship might not have an end, Megan's life had taught her to always be prepared. Despite Harry's optimism, she knew she couldn't let herself be unprepared—just in case—for the possibility of the wonderful magic ending when Monday came and they returned to Saint Louis.

When real life intruded, with all of its problems scattering the beautiful dream, Megan knew she could only depend on herself in the end. She had to be prepared, for she was always the one others, especially her mother, depended on. Megan had to remain a rock.

But that didn't mean she'd give up on Harry and the now that they had. She just was a realist enough to know not to hold him to promises of ever after.

But wouldn't it be nice to be Mrs. Harry Sanders? She'd wake up every morning in his arms. They could drive to work together and...

Wait. She didn't even know where he lived, much less what type of car he drove. Something sporty and flashy probably. Abruptly she pushed those annoying and disturbing thoughts out of her head. Time for those much later. Live in the now.

"Thanks for taking me sight-seeing," she said, searching for a safe topic. "I've had a great time."

"I'll admit, it's probably the best idea my grandfather ever had," Harry said.

He paused. Megan's eyebrows had knit slightly together, and the expression on her face was one of curiosity and confusion. Her expression had him making an instant decision. She had the right to know. He smoothed out her forehead with his finger before leaning over and dropping a brief kiss on the top of her cute nose. He then took a deep breath before beginning.

"I guess I need to tell you this so you won't be totally taken off guard when my grandfather arrives tomorrow. Grandpa Joe is quite a piece of work, and believe me, he can be formidable."

Harry began to trace Megan's jawbone with the back of his hand. Her skin was soft and silky to the touch. "My grandfather is the ultimate in meddling matchmakers. I'm sure you heard the story of my sister Darci and how he 'helped' her out with Cameron."

Megan moved more toward him as Harry continued to stroke her face. Her skin felt so smooth, so right under his attentions. "Anyway, I have absolutely no doubt in my mind that when my grandfather chose me to be your mentor that he was hoping exactly what happened between us last night would happen. He's insinuated to me as much many a time."

"Oh," Megan said. Her brown eyes widened and

Harry couldn't help himself. He moved his hand and began to trace her soft eyebrows with his forefinger.

"That's why I was so upset last night when I found out he sent the theater tickets. It had nothing to do with you, but more just me being angry at him. He's always putting people in situations they can't get out of right away. He calls it a helpful nudge. He's quite good at it. He did it with Darci when he told her to be Cameron's tour guide. In fact, my sister thinks I'm next on Grandpa Joe's get-the-grandchildren-married quest."

"I see." Megan shrugged and pulled away a little. "You don't have to worry about me, Harry. I'm not out to snag a husband from this trip to New York."

Ouch. Obviously he wasn't being clear.

Harry gathered Megan to his chest and pushed on. He had to make her understand. "Megan, I hate it when my grandfather's right, when he sees things that I don't. We've always been at too many cross-purposes. But he did thrust me into the role of your mentor."

He took a deep breath. The next words were crucial. "No matter what, Megan, please know that I certainly did not fall into bed with you because my grandfather hoped it would happen. Much to his disappointment, he's never dictated what I do. I wanted you, heck, I want you right now, just because you are you."

"Oh," was about all Megan could manage as she tried to absorb it all. Joe Jacobsen had been playing matchmaker. But why her? She was a nobody in Saint

Louis society—well, any society for that matter. She and Harry came from different worlds, different lifestyles. But for right now, Harry still wanted her. She'd never understand it, but after last night she couldn't deny that she felt the same way. She wanted him right back.

As if sensing the myriad thoughts dancing in the silence between them, Harry leaned forward and brought his lips to hers. The immediate haven Megan found in his kiss washed over her, sending the debilitating doubts scurrying back to the far cobwebbed recesses of her brain. She opened her mouth to him, drinking deeply of the magic elixir she now needed to stay whole.

For maybe Harry might fall in love with her. Maybe he might not ever want to leave her. Maybe she could keep a man like Harry Sanders happy for the rest of his days.

Something about the sounds of jogging feet caused her to break from his kiss. A couple, running in unison, approached. It took Megan a moment to place them from their photographs, and then she knew exactly which international celebrities they were.

"Harry, look! That's—it's on the tip of my tongue—oh, right," Megan named the couple as she watched them jog off. "Wait until my mother hears that I saw them."

Megan's smile was infectious and Harry smiled in spite of the fact that he had no clue as to who Megan was talking about. Sad, perhaps, but then he'd never been a royalty watcher of any country. He did, thanks to a high school geography teacher, at least know where the tiny European country was.

"I didn't know royalty went jogging," Harry finally remarked.

"Well, she's always been different," Megan said. "She's a jewelry designer and always lived her life the way she wanted to and not quite the way a princess should. For her the heart is always more important. Did you know her husband is nineteen years older than she is?"

Harry shook his head as Megan continued. "My mom closely followed all the marriage follies of this side of the royal family."

"So your mom is into royal watching."

Megan nodded, her brown hair bobbing around her chin. Harry reached forward and pushed a loose strand back behind her right ear. The lock was silky to his touch.

"Mom's crazy about royals," Megan said. "She even buys the tabloids so she can read about them, and she'd devoured all the biographies."

"So you're a royalty watcher too?"

Megan's face broke into a slightly guilty, yet playful, smile. "Not really. I mostly follow their lives just to make conversation with my mom. Although, I admit, like every little girl I always wanted to be a princess."

She paused a moment as the memories overtook her. Then she briskly said, "But of course what little girl doesn't fantasize about that growing up? We all dream of our handsome prince sweeping in on his white horse just like in every fairy tale that there is.''

''I always wanted a black horse,'' Harry said, lightening the mood and moment slightly. He kissed the tip of Megan's addicting nose again. ''Do you know, can a prince have a black or brown horse?''

''I guess so,'' Megan replied.

''Good, because I've always been partial to Thoroughbred horses,'' Harry said. ''I even own a stake in one. It'll run in the Kentucky Derby next year.''

''Really,'' Megan said.

Harry laughed. ''Yes, really, although I'll admit, I just own a small stake. An old college buddy of mine from Vanderbilt married a woman whose family trains and races horses. When they were looking for investors for this new colt, I bought in. He has loads of potential both on the track and, if he wins, later as a stud. Anyhow, next May, I'm going to Churchill Downs for the race.''

''That sounds awesome,'' Megan said. ''I used to watch the horses run when I was in sixth grade. You know, when all girls want horses.''

''It should be an interesting time. If you've ever read a Dick Francis mystery you know horse racing is a world unto itself with a protocol like none other. Of course my grandfather thinks the whole horse thing is nonsense and a waste of money, but after all, it's my money to waste.''

''Excuse me for being so bold, but you and your grandfather don't seem to have the most stable relationship,'' Megan said. ''Sorry for the pun.''

"No problem," Harry replied. He thought for a moment about what Megan had said. Was his relationship with his grandfather stable at all? Probably not, Harry reflected. Even though each did care about the other, they'd never really seen eye to eye. Ever.

"Let's just say that being family is probably all we have in common," Harry said. "He's not really pleased with much that I do. I mean, just look at me. He should have filled Darci's empty spot by making me vice president of development. Like that happened. But I'm hoping that finally, after I return from this trip, he'll promote me. I've waited long enough."

Harry paused for a moment to finger another loose strand of her hair. "Of course, when he discovers we've hit it off he'll be delighted. God, Megan, I'm sorry to drag you into this. He's going to be unbearable once he realizes we're involved."

"While I didn't know the risks going in, you, Harry Sanders, are worth it."

And as Megan spoke the words she knew how true they really were. Harry was worth it. He was worth any risk she would have to take, any hardships she might endure during the course of whatever relationship they carved out. She loved him too much not to be with him.

She placed her hands on his and leaned over to kiss him. "We'll take it as it comes, okay?"

"Okay," Harry said, letting himself slide into the delightful abyss of her kiss. He was finding himself wanting her more and more. As his lips caressed hers, he knew that with Megan he would never be bored.

He wouldn't feel stifled or trapped. He wouldn't slake lust and want to fly away as he'd done so many times before.

Megan was like home, like a place of nurture. She fit him, she made him a better man. At this moment he couldn't see ever wanting to let her go.

Except for temporarily as he reached for the cell phone that had begun shrilling in his pocket. Seeing the New York City area code he grimaced. "Hello, Darci," he said. "You always have impeccable timing."

"Don't give me any grief, brother dear," his sister said with a laugh. "How am I to know what you're doing, and here I am trying to save you from restaurant food. Anyway, I tried the hotel first but you weren't there. You aren't there, are you?"

"No, I'm out," Harry said. He played with Megan's fingertips. Was Darci saying something? Harry tried to focus as Megan lifted one of his fingers to her lips and kissed the end.

"Cameron and I've decided to grill on the terrace," Darci said. "Come on over. I won't see you for a while after you leave Monday."

"I'm sight-seeing," Harry replied, although the sun had just begun to set.

"Bring her along. You've got Megan with you, don't you?"

Did his sister have a crystal ball? "Yes," Harry said.

"So bring her. It'll make a foursome for cards. I want to meet her. You caved in, didn't you?"

"That's none of your business," Harry retorted. Megan's eyebrows arched her unspoken question. My sister, Harry mouthed.

Darci's laughter echoed through the phone. "You did, didn't you? I know you too well. So bring her over. I want to meet her, especially if she's as special as you said she was the other night. You're not afraid to introduce her to me, are you? Well, are you?"

Was he? He held the phone to his ear and moved his free hand from Megan's fingertips to again trace her lips. She was so special, so perfect. He wanted to keep her to himself, all to himself, but he knew that wasn't fair to Megan. She didn't need to feel the complex of being "hidden," of not being good enough to meet the family.

"We're in Central Park now. We'll be there in ten minutes."

"Excellent," Darci said. "I'll have Cameron heat up the grill."

Harry ended the phone call. "My sister has just summoned us for dinner," he told Megan. "Is that okay with you?"

"Yes," Megan said. "You need to spend time with her."

"Actually, she'll probably want to spend more time with you so that she can pick your brain as to what you're doing with me."

"I'll tell her it's because you're so good in bed," Megan said with a devilish smile.

"You wouldn't dare," Harry said, carrying her joke further. She was joking, wasn't she?

"Why not when it's the truth?"

"You evil woman," Harry said. All she had to do was speak and he wanted her. "Temptress."

Darci and the impromptu dinner party could wait for a little while longer, just as Harry would need to wait until later tonight to fully give in to the temptation that was Megan. But for right now he could at least get a taste of the magical night to come.

As the sun drifted down beyond the Manhattan skyline, Harry swooped down to kiss Megan's lips again.

"HI, MEGAN, I'M DARCI. It's so nice to finally meet you."

Megan reached her hand forward, shaking Darci's outstretched one. "Hi," she said, suddenly shy.

"Do come in," Darci said, stepping back from the doorway to her Central Park West apartment.

As Megan stepped into the apartment, her first thought was how huge the rooms were. The foyer itself was as big as all the rooms in Megan's flat put together. With its wide circular staircase leading to an upper floor, the marble-floored foyer was an architectural marvel.

So this was how the other half lived. As she and Harry followed Darci through the marble columns flanking the archway in the great room, suddenly Megan's insecurities and doubts assailed her.

What was she doing here? She couldn't play in this sandbox—she couldn't afford even the rent for a closet. Did Harry live in a place this size?

What did she really know about Harry, or his life-style, anyway? Absolutely nothing.

As if sensing that her nervous system was over-loading, Harry tightened his grip on Megan's hand. "This is my husband, Cameron," Darci said.

"Nice to meet you, Megan." Cameron offered his hand, and Megan somehow managed to make her grip as firm and steady as his as she took his hand. Cameron O'Brien, one of the richest men on the planet and also one of the most powerful, had just welcomed little nobody Megan MacGregor into his gorgeously decorated home.

The thought that she was standing here in this room with these people was surreal. She wouldn't be here if it weren't for Harry. She understood business, but this was a new playing field altogether. It was personal.

And they'd genuinely welcomed her just because Harry thought her special.

Megan took a moment to glance at Harry as Darci bustled about getting cocktails. Even though Cameron O'Brien had always been one of the most handsome men in the world, Megan realized that to her, Harry was the more attractive of the two.

Although both were blond, Harry stood taller. His face crinkled into those delightful lines when he laughed. And his lips, those full lips always called to her in a way that no other had ever managed to do.

Darci handed Megan a glass of white wine. "Is this okay?" she asked. "Harry told me white wine is your favorite and this is my personal favorite."

"Thank you," Megan said as she accepted the wineglass. She took a tiny sip. The flavors rolled over her tongue and danced their way down her throat. Wow. For a moment Megan considered asking Darci about the wine, but reality stopped her. It didn't matter what vineyard bottled this masterful beverage. Megan knew she couldn't afford this particular vintage in a million years.

In fact, as the night wore on, Megan found herself more and more torn. Darci and Cameron were down-to-earth people, but the underlying presence of being a "have" was always there. It was ingrained; a personal comfort in knowing that one never had to worry about money.

Megan's life couldn't have been more different, and as much as she wanted to relate, she couldn't. Any extra income didn't go for things like artwork, a fancier television, designer furniture. Most of Megan's things were secondhand, her flat tiny, her food the generic store brands. Every extra penny she could squeeze out went into a savings account earmarked for paying her mother's doctors for the upcoming medical treatment.

But for Harry's sake, she tried to enjoy herself, and as she did genuinely like Darci, it was easy to find common footing when discussing things like national politics, the latest movies and baseball. Being from Saint Louis herself, home of the beloved Saint Louis Cardinals baseball team, Darci still couldn't find herself rooting for the New York Mets.

"It's a bone of contention between me and Cameron," Darci confided to Megan as they sat on the terrace. "I can at least root for the Yankees. After all, they're an American League team, not National, and Joe Torre was once a Cardinals player. Even though he didn't last as the Cardinals's manager, Saint Louis was thrilled for his back-to-back World Series wins."

"Right," Megan said, "we root for the Yankees unless they're playing us."

"Exactly," Darci said.

Cameron leaned over toward his wife. "Are you bashing my Mets again?" he asked. "They aren't pond scum like you Saint Louis people claim."

"I never said they were, dear," Darci replied with a wink in Megan's direction.

Darci stood, her figure silhouetted from the hidden lights that made the terrace dark and shadowy, yet still bright enough to see food and dinner companions. "I'm going to retrieve our dessert." She reached for Megan's empty dinner plate. "Harry, why don't you help me?"

"Because I'm a guest?" Harry replied, trying to wiggle out of the task.

But an instant undercurrent passed between the two and Megan watched in fascination as Harry rose to his feet and grabbed some of the dirty plates. Within moments, Megan was alone with Cameron.

"So you like him?" Cameron asked.

Megan reached for her wineglass, the only thing around to hold in order to hide her shaking nerves. "I do," Megan replied.

"He doesn't scare you?" Cameron leaned back in his chair.

"No," Megan said. "I've never been scared of him, not as a person. I've done several business battles with him, and even he'll tell you that I'm not afraid to go head-to-head with him. Honestly, though, since I know what you're really after, whatever this thing is between us, that's what petrifies me to death."

Cameron chuckled, a warm, pleased sound that indicated his approval of her answer. "You're a wise woman to recognize that."

"I don't know about calling myself wise. I fell for him, didn't I?" Megan gestured around the terrace. "I certainly don't live in this kind of world."

"I've learned that for the most part worlds are the same," Cameron said. He twirled his wineglass that had long gone empty. "It's the emotions that matter, not what social status or items people have. Trust me, Darci taught me that. It's what's underneath the exterior that really counts. Although, yes, having money helps. Especially in Harry's case, for if you ever get to the point of living with Harry, you'll be glad he can afford a maid. According to Darci, her brother is an absolute slob and has no idea how to clean a thing."

Cameron saw her look. "Okay, and neither do I."

Megan laughed. "Maybe it is just a guy thing."

"Maybe," Cameron conceded, and from there they started talking about Megan's latest business projects, and under Cameron's skillful questioning, she warmed to the topic and found herself enjoying the rest of the conversation a great deal.

But a part of her still wondered, just what were Harry and Darci talking about anyway?

Chapter Ten

"She's a gem," Darci said. She'd called Harry into the kitchen not because she needed any help, but rather because she wanted to pick his brain.

She poked her head out through the French doors and then withdrew it back again before either Cameron or Megan could see her. "I'll have to admit it, Grandpa Joe made a good choice for you. I like her."

"I like her too," Harry admitted as he stacked the dirty dishes on the counter. "You know how it is with me, Darci."

"What, love 'em and leave 'em?" Darci teased.

Harry leaned back against the counter. How true that was, at least before. But now, after Megan, he'd realized why.

"Well, they end up boring me. I'm not a stupid man, Darci. Oh, don't give me that look. I know you don't think I am. I'm just making a point. A guy has to be able to talk to a woman about something more than what nail color she's wearing."

Darci held up her hand. "What, you don't like Ravish Me Red?"

Harry shot her a "please" look. "You know what I mean, Darci. While a woman may be beautiful and the lights may be on, inside there's no one home. I've dated enough of them to know that I don't want one of those women long term. They're arm ornaments. They look pretty. But I can't imagine spending any real time with them or even holding a real conversation with them about something that matters."

"Go on," Darci said. She reached for a stack of dessert plates and set them on a tray.

"Megan, she's different. She's not afraid to argue to my face. She's got ideas that build on mine, or mine build on hers, and she's sharp as a tack. There's something about her that puts all of the others to shame. She's got something inside." He made a fist and tapped his chest for emphasis.

"So you've found your match," Darci said. She set four silver dessert forks on the tray. "I'm so happy for you."

"But how do you know the love won't vanish? How do you know it won't just disappear one night?"

Darci paused from taking the cake out of the refrigerator. She simply held the door open, not caring that the appliance was chilling the room.

"Love is a choice, Harry. You choose to love someone through thick and thin, better or worse. You know that this is the person you'll sacrifice everything for. That's how you know it's real. That's how you know it's right. That person is your absolute number-one priority. They come before everything else.''

And with that she shut the refrigerator door and walked over to Harry. She stretched out her arms. She hadn't hugged him in a long time, probably since their paternal grandfather had died over ten years ago, and now was as good a time as any to start hugging again.

''It's scary, and, you know, at times love can hurt like hell. Just take it slow. Take it fast if that makes you feel better. But whatever you do, know that you're going to have to take risks. Gambles.''

''I don't think I've ever gambled this way,'' Harry said into his sister's shoulder. Her hug was filled with emotional support.

''You haven't. Emotional gambles are so different from the riskiest business ventures. It's flying blind. You'll have to always be honest with each other. You always have to communicate. And that's hard. You won't know how she feels unless she tells you, or if you tell her how you feel. If she rejects you, it's better to know now before you've built up years of dreams on an illusion.''

''Let her not be an illusion,'' Harry said.

''I don't think she is, if that helps,'' Darci said.

She released Harry from the hug and gazed up into the Jacobsen blue eyes that were like looking at her own in a mirror. ''I think you've found her.''

I do too. Harry let those words remain unspoken. ''Shall we get back out there?''

''Absolutely. You take the tray and I'll carry the

cake. It's coconut. Your favorite if I remember right. I made it myself.''

Harry watched as Darci retrieved the cake. ''Since when did you learn how to cook?''

''I've always known how to cook. I did sneak into our kitchen on many occasion and our cook taught me a few little things. But, I'll admit, since I've been married I've been taking some classes here and there. My last one was cakes. I get tired of eating out, and although we can afford it, I don't want a housekeeper underfoot all the time. I still like to be able to be spontaneous with my husband.''

''Eww,'' Harry said in a laughing tone as he balanced the tray and walked toward the French doors. ''TMI. Too much information, sister dear.''

Darci laughed as she followed him out through the double doors.

''YOU MADE THIS YOURSELF? It's delicious,'' Megan said as she accepted a second small sliver of Darci's coconut cake. ''I'm partial to chocolate myself, but I'll admit, this comes a close second.''

''You like chocolate, huh?'' Harry teased.

''What woman doesn't?'' Cameron added.

''Exactly,'' Megan said.

She waved her fork for a moment before scooping up another morsel of the delicious cake. ''My mother's fiancé, Bill, is one of the bartenders at Henrietta's and he often brings Mom dinner. When he does, he always brings me a slice of the chocolate suicide cake.''

"I'll have to make Claire give me that recipe," Darci declared.

"Cousinly rivalry," Cameron joked.

"You could probably give her this one in trade," Harry said as he forked another bite of his third piece of cake into his mouth. When he finished swallowing, he said, "Henrietta's could use a cake like this, even if it is just a seasonal menu item."

"This cake is definitely good enough," Darci declared. "I even baked the coconut myself. I drained the juice, broke the coconut open with a hammer, and then scooped out the meat."

"You sound like the Little Red Hen," Cameron said, teasing his wife about the hen that made the loaf of bread all by herself.

Harry laughed. "Better watch it, Cameron, she is a Jacobsen descendant and you know how our family is about food. She may not feed you for days."

"Yeah," Darci agreed.

Cameron leaned over and dipped his right forefinger into Darci's icing. He brought it to her lips. "Then I'll have to feed you."

As Darci fixated on Cameron and taking the sinful white morsel from his fingertips, Harry reached over and covered Megan's hand with his own. He leaned toward her and whispered, "Five minutes?"

She smiled, immediately understanding Harry's intent on leaving the two lovebirds alone. "I think that sounds good."

Harry leaned back in his chair and coughed slightly, the sound breaking Cameron and Darci's monopoly of each other. "We need to get going back to the hotel," Harry said as Darci pulled back from her husband.

Darci blinked as she focused on Harry. "So soon? We didn't play cards yet. It's just barely eleven."

"True, but you don't have the old guy descending on you at some unknown time tomorrow afternoon."

"Oh." Darci's face fell into resigned understanding. "Grandpa Joe's coming in for the press conference."

"Yes, and Megan and I need to be on our toes. No dark circles allowed underneath our eyes."

"No kidding. I love him dearly, but he can be such a bear. What do you think of our grandfather, Megan?"

Megan folded her hands into her lap. "I guess I don't see him the way you do. He's always been really nice to me and given me all sorts of fantastic opportunities. But then, he's not my family. Harry's told me about him. I suspect since I'm not family, the expectations he has for me are a lot different."

"Spoken like a true diplomat," Cameron said. "The man's a dynamo...that one thing is for sure."

"He definitely is," Darci said. "But he's usually right about most things, as much as we—" Darci looked at Harry "—hate to admit it. Well, let's get you out of here so you don't get on his bad side tomorrow."

And with that the evening drew to an end. Within minutes everyone had said their goodbyes. "Don't be a stranger,'' Darci told Harry as she gave him a good-bye hug.

Darci gave Megan a hug too, pulling her aside so the men wouldn't hear. ''You take care of Harry,'' Darci warned. ''He's a sensitive one deep down.''

''I will,'' Megan promised. She then allowed Harry to lead her from the apartment and soon they were in a cab headed back toward their hotel.

''It was a good night,'' Megan said.

''I'm glad,'' Harry said.

''You have a wonderful family,'' Megan said. ''I'll admit, after seeing you with Darci, part of me wishes I had a sibling.''

''I guess there are good and bad parts to it.'' Harry began to toy with Megan's fingertips. He laced his hand through hers and brought her fingertips up to meet his lips. ''She liked you.''

''She did?''

''She did,'' Harry said. He threaded his hands into Megan's face and drew her head toward his. ''Not as much as me, though.''

''Really?''

''Uh-huh,'' Harry said as he lowered his lips to hers. The kiss he gave her was gentle and tender, and Megan allowed herself to be drawn deeper into the magic that was Harry Sanders. Neither noticed that the cab had drawn up into the circle driveway of the hotel.

''Marriott East Side,'' the cabbie announced.

As the doorman opened her door, only then did she and Harry break apart, Megan's face a telltale flush from being well kissed. She waited for Harry by the entrance doors, and within moments after Harry paid the driver, no words were needed as they crossed the lobby and caught an elevator upstairs to their floor.

"My place or yours?" Harry teased as he broke the silence.

Megan turned to face him. "You know, I don't even know where you live."

They stepped out of the elevator and Harry inserted his passkey into his hotel room door. He turned the handle after the light flashed green. "I have a condo in one of the high-rises on Hanley Road in Clayton," he said. "I look east toward the Arch."

"Oh."

"Oh no. It's not like Cameron and Darci's place. That's ostentatious. Mine is nothing fancy, just a small one-bedroom unit."

Harry guided her inside the hotel room. The maid had already turned down the sheets and had placed two mints on the pillows. "Think nine hundred square feet and that's it. It's one of the smaller units in the building. It seemed a good investment that I could rent out down the road when I buy a house, and so I bought it from my cousin Nick when he moved to Chicago."

He paused, seeing her look. Time to put her mind at rest. "And it's not a playboy den either. Over ninety percent of the people living in my building are retired or just about to be. I'll definitely show it to you when we get back, okay?"

"Okay." Megan smiled and looked up at the man

she loved. He was so beautiful, and yet again he'd surprised her. No playboy den for Harry. Her respect and love for him grew even more, if that were possible.

"Just remember, Megan, you can always ask me anything," Harry said.

He put both hands on her shoulders and drew her next to him. "I don't want there to be any secrets and insecurities between us, Megan. We can take this slow, we can take this fast."

He tightened his grip and pulled her even closer next to him. "But we have to communicate. We always have to be honest with each other. At least that's what Darci said when she and I were in the kitchen. She was chock-full of advice and she had no hesitation in sharing it."

"Well, she is happy," Megan replied.

The love that Darci and Cameron shared had been more than obvious. Darci had simply glowed with the way she felt for her husband. Her husband certainly didn't hide his feelings either.

Harry began to knead the back of Megan's shoulders and she relaxed. Harry was such a special man, and the warmth radiating from Harry's chest felt so good, so right. Raw heat began to pool in her lower belly. Never would she stop wanting this man.

"They both are very happy," Harry said. "And we will be too." And with that he lowered his mouth, bringing his lips down to kiss hers.

The kiss said everything else that needed to be said, holding the representative emotional promise of words that were too soon to be said aloud. Harry deepened the kiss, sending Megan into breathless anticipation.

Tonight Harry was in no mood for slow, and Megan reveled in more of Harry's lovemaking that always sent her spiraling into the magical beyond.

Clothes flew into far corners, hands caressed and aroused, and finally bodies intertwined and molded together—preordained since time began to fit perfectly and bring rapturous harmony.

Afterward Megan simply lay across Harry, her ear pressed against his chest. Her body spent, she listened to his breathing as it became slow, steady and regular as his heart rate returned to normal.

She could spend every day, every night like this if it meant being in Harry's arms. Life, at this moment, was absolutely perfect.

Sure, he hadn't said the words declaring endless love and neither had she, but it didn't matter. Subconsciously she could feel that he cared about her, and she knew that she loved him with all her heart. For now that was more than enough.

They were two halves that together made a perfect whole.

She could tell when he drifted off to sleep and then she let a wide smile claim her. She let the feelings of happiness wash over her. The joy she felt tingled all the away down to her toes.

Without a doubt, after a brief rest, he'd wake up later in the night, and wanting her again, once more they'd come together. She closed her eyes, letting the blissful darkness soothe her soul.

She'd need her rest for that lovemaking too. When it came to Harry she'd discovered she was quite insatiable. She loved him. She wanted to be in his arms all the time.

Yes, life was indeed perfect and she made a sudden vow to herself to refuse to let anything, including the arrival of Grandpa Joe or the subsequent return to Saint Louis spoil it.

Nothing would spoil it. Ever. She wouldn't let it, not when she'd found the man of her dreams.

His heart beat steady against her ear, she shifted deeper into his arms and fell fast asleep.

Chapter Eleven

Breakfast was the complimentary room service bagels and coffee that Harry carried from the living area and served to Megan in bed. He'd even made her hot chocolate. Never had food tasted so good, Megan marveled. After a night and a morning of lovemaking, at two in the afternoon she was starved.

"It's a good thing you're wearing clothes," Harry said as he fed her a last bite of a strawberry cream cheese covered bagel. She licked the creamy pink remnants off his finger. "Stop that or I might have to eat you instead."

"Ah, promises." Megan slapped away the different finger he was moving under the spaghetti strap of her camisole top. She'd retrieved the outfit from her room earlier that morning. If Grandpa Joe showed up early, at least she wouldn't be caught naked.

"Later," she admonished as she moved Harry's wandering fingers.

"Ah, later." Harry sobered for a moment. He moved his hands back into his personal space before reaching on the bedside table for his coffee. "I wish. My grandfather's arriving today. He'll definitely be putting a dent in things, believe me. Playtime will probably have to be postponed."

"So what will our schedule be?"

"I don't really know. He likes to be eccentric, that's for sure. Instead of giving me an itinerary, he just said he'd be arriving into town sometime this afternoon. He could be here now for all I know. He didn't really say what we'd be doing or when we'd be meeting with him if at all. I'm assuming that at the minimum we'll have to do some sort of debriefing with him, and I'm not sure if he's going to see Darci or not."

"Is your grandfather always this complicated?"

"Yes. The man is a genius when it comes to business, but sometimes when it comes to family I think he's got a screw or two loose in terms of common courtesy and sense. While he means well, he definitely marches to his own drummer."

Megan finished the last of her bagel. "Maybe he won't contact us at all if he's being a matchmaker. He'll want us to remain alone. You know, in bed. Hmm. Now there's a pleasant thought."

Harry's expression grew wistful. "I wish. There's nothing more I'd like better. I'd love to stay in bed with you all day."

Harry reached out and stroked the side of Megan's face. She blushed, making her even more beautiful. His body quickened and he tamped down his desire. When Grandpa Joe was involved, one couldn't be caught unawares.

"No, unfortunately bed will have to wait. One thing's for certain. My grandfather is going to want to know what's going on as soon as he arrives. In fact, I wouldn't put it past him to have bribed housekeeping to give him the status of our sheets upon his arrival."

"Well, whatever it is that he's up to, we'll handle it together," Megan said. She finished the last of her orange juice and set the glass aside. "I suppose that means we do have to get showered."

Harry didn't like that idea. He frowned. "I guess it is time to join the real world for a little while."

He looked so bummed out that Megan leaned over and kissed him. Although she didn't want to, she knew better than to linger and thus she withdrew her lips quickly. Harry was too much of a temptation wearing nothing but a pair of silk boxer shorts. Neither of them needed to be caught in bed when his grandfather arrived, and if she kissed him any more she wouldn't be able to stop.

She wiggled out from under the covers. "I'm going to my room to shower. How about I meet you in a few?"

"Since that's the only choice I get, I guess it's fine," Harry said as he watched her leave the room. She had such a magical hold over him. Even after that brief a kiss, he'd need the cold shower just to regroup.

MEGAN SHOWERED faster than usual. She wasn't exactly sure why, but it had something to do with Harry.

She didn't want to be without him, even for a moment. The phone in her bedroom rang.

"Hello?"

"Megan, Joe Jacobsen here. How are you?"

"I'm fine, sir," Megan said. She sat down on her bed, glad she was already dressed in linen trousers and a silk blouse. Her hair, as usual, she let air dry.

Joe's voice sounded crisp. "I'm glad to hear you're doing well. What about my grandson? I've tried him and he's not answering."

"He's in the shower, I believe," Megan replied.

"That explains it. Anyway, I'm here." He rattled off a suite number. "Since you're obviously ready, why don't you come right up? There are a few matters I'd like to discuss with you."

Megan twisted the phone cord around her finger. "Well, I told Harry I'd meet him and—"

"That's what message lights and paper are for. I'd prefer a few moments of your time alone if possible. Now would be best, Megan."

How to argue with that? His summons was crystal clear. "I'll be right up." She untangled her finger and replaced the receiver.

She put her shoes on and went into Harry's room. She could hear the water running in the bathroom. Shyness overtook her for a moment, for when had she ever walked in on Harry? Then, gathering her wits, she knocked boldly and opened the door. After all, she'd definitely seen him naked.

"Harry?"

"Come to join me, darling?"

The thought sent wanton shivers through her. From their shower together yesterday she already had a vivid mental picture of what the water cascading over Harry's hard lean body looked like. And when he'd made love to her under the droplets...

"I wish. Your grandfather just called. He's here and he wants me up there now."

"Typical. He wants everyone to dance to his tune."

"Anyway, I'm going to go on up." Megan gave Harry the room number. He suddenly poked his head around the curtain. Droplets of water cascaded from his blond hair and clung to his eyelashes.

"You were going to give me a kiss, weren't you?"

Never one to forgo one of Harry's kisses, Megan stepped closer. "Only if you don't get me wet."

"Well, not with water anyway," Harry teased. He kissed her briefly and wanting more, Megan reluctantly drew back. As promised, no water had touched her clothes.

"I've got to shave and then I'll be up. About twenty minutes tops."

"I'll see you there." Megan stepped out of the steamy bathroom and within moments was in the elevator heading for Joe Jacobsen's floor.

His suite was the same layout as hers and Harry's except that his suite had only one bedroom attached to it.

"Come in," he said as he opened the door. He gestured toward a chair. "You look lovely as ever."

"Thank you," Megan said. She sat primly on her

hands. Knowing Harry was still to arrive, she wasn't surprised that Joe Jacobsen left the door to the suite propped open by using the metal safety lock as a wedge.

"Can I get you anything? Water? Soft drink? Something to eat?"

"Water is fine," Megan said. She watched as Joe pulled a bottle of Evian out of the minibar. "Did you have a nice flight?"

"Uneventful," Joe said. "The new security measures take a little more time, but flying first class alleviates a lot of that. You get your own security gate."

"I found that helpful," Megan said.

"So, flight aside, how have you liked New York?"

"I've enjoyed it, but not enough to live here. The play was excellent. Thank you for the tickets."

"You're welcome." Joe chuckled, his beard bobbing slightly. "Ah, and don't worry. You're too valuable in the home office for me to transfer you anywhere. Besides, no point. You won't leave your mother."

"No, sir, I wouldn't."

"I like that." Joe's beard bobbed as he motioned his approval of her answer. "Loyalty. You've got a lot of fine qualities. I've always been impressed with you, Megan, and you haven't disappointed me on this business trip. I knew I was right to assign you to the team. Your ideas saved the Evie's acquisition."

"Thank you for the compliment. I mean, I try to be a good—"

Joe cut her off. "Oh, your work performance is never in question. My crystal ball sees you having a long tenure with Jacobsen Enterprises with or without my grandson's opinion. Speaking of Harry, tell me, do you love him?"

"What?" Megan sat there, stunned. So strong was her reaction that luckily she'd just finished a sip of water. If not, it might have sputtered its way back up through her nose or something horrid like that. Joe Jacobsen had definitely caught her off guard. "Sir, I..."

Joe chuckled again before he reached over and patted her hand reassuringly. "Now, now. Just look at you. I'm not a mind reader or anything, but I have been told I can read people. You, my dear, have become involved with my grandson in ways other than strictly business."

Did he really know? Could he really tell? Or was he bluffing and fishing for confirmation? Megan had no way of being certain. How should she answer his questions? She wished Harry would hurry up and arrive. He'd know what to do.

"Megan, do you love my grandson? The truth would be good here." His blue eyes locked onto hers as if trying to pry into her innermost thoughts. Silence grew as he waited.

But after all, did the answer really matter? Would telling him make a difference? What call should she make? "Yes," she finally answered honestly. "I do."

"And does he love you?"

Megan twisted her hands in her lap. "That I don't know."

Joe nodded as if he expected that answer from her. "He always was a fool of a boy. I'm going to have to do something about that."

Megan straightened up. Harry had called his Grandpa Joe a meddler, but this was her life, hers and Harry's. Joe Jacobsen had done enough. "No, you don't."

Joe's eyes darkened, becoming almost entirely the color of the dark rim of blue. He looked totally surprised by her outburst.

"Sir, no offense meant, but please stay out. This is my life and Harry's and we can handle it. I've heard what a matchmaker you are, and all about your helpful nudges. But we don't need any. We're both consenting, communicating adults. We can take it from here."

His chin lifted and he peered over at her. "You think?"

"I know," Megan said. She held her spine rigid and she gripped her hands tightly in her lap. She'd just pretty much told her company CEO to take a hike and mind his own business. Now what would he do? Hopefully not fire her. He'd just said he thought she had a long tenure at Jacobsen Enterprises. Of course, that had been before she'd admitted she loved Harry.

To her surprise, Joe did nothing that she expected. Instead he started laughing. "You are his perfect match. I knew it. Only you can get right back on him, just as you did me right now. I knew you were the one.'' He slapped his knees and drew a deep, calming breath. "Pardon me. I promise not to intrude any further into your personal life.''

"Thank you,'' Megan said. Wariness still filled her. Instinct told her that Joe Jacobsen wasn't finished yet with whatever he'd planned.

"There is a caveat, though. I am allowed to meddle in my business affairs, pun intended. You, my dear, have done everything I've asked you and more this past year. And these past few weeks you've gone above and beyond. Like I said, you saved Evie's. Even better, you've put up with Harry and that's no small feat in itself. I'm extremely impressed that you've managed to partner him so well in all areas. With your influence Harry has done things this trip that he'd never have done in a million years had you not suggested them.''

"It's not all me, sir. You really need to give Harry a lot more credit than—''

Joe ignored her interruption and kept right on going. "Whatever. I don't care about Harry. It's you right now that I'm concerned with. You're being promoted as soon as we return. How does vice president of development sound?''

"Well, I—''

But Grandpa Joe was not to be stopped by any objections she might have. "It comes with quite a hefty pay raise, which, I believe, you could put to good use with your mother's upcoming treatment. Didn't it get moved up? Doesn't it start next week?''

"Yes, Tuesday, but—'' Megan blinked. How had

Joe known about her mother? ''Really, I don't know what to say except that I'm honored.''

Joe leaned forward, cutting off anything else she might add. ''It's pretty simple, Megan. All you have to do is say yes.''

But Megan couldn't make the words come. Something was terribly wrong. She could feel it. Right now she should be jumping for joy. She'd been handed the promotion of her dreams, yet instead of happiness, her internal radar was on full alert and screaming danger.

She glanced up and everything became crystal clear. Harry stood in the doorway, his face a livid mask of pure rage.

''I got ready faster than I thought,'' he said.

HARRY HAD WHISTLED most of the elevator ride. Now he wondered why he had bothered. The last few minutes had seemed like a bad dream. Upon reaching the suite, he'd found the doorway open, and so he'd stepped inside. When he'd heard Grandpa Joe speaking, Harry had paused. He'd learned long ago not to interrupt his grandfather.

The words he'd overheard, though, hadn't been complimentary. Far from it. First Grandpa Joe had praised Megan for partnering Harry. Then he'd called her the reason for Harry's success. But the rest of the words had truly crushed him.

''I don't care about Harry,'' Grandpa Joe had said. ''It's you right now that I'm concerned with. You're being promoted as soon as we return. How does vice president of development sound?''

His grandfather had just filled the position, a position that should have been his. He'd given it to Megan. Once again Harry hadn't been good enough. Even worse, the love of his life had just sat there with a stunned look on her face and told Grandpa Joe that she was honored.

But who could blame her? Getting promoted was an honor, and in the end, maybe he had been right about Megan all along. When it came right down to it, the only thing in her life that was really important was herself, that and taking care of her mother. As Grandpa Joe had said, her new raise would help along that end quite nicely.

''Congratulations,'' he said stiffly.

''Harry, I didn't—''

He cut her off. He didn't want to hear any lies, any excuses. ''Save it, Megan. Save it for someone who cares. Save it for someone who gives a damn. You got a promotion for being able to handle me.''

''That's not—''

''Spare me,'' Harry said. ''I don't think I could stomach any more. Did you and my grandfather cook this all up?'' He turned to Grandpa Joe. ''Maybe she didn't, but you sure did. You probably had this all planned out weeks ago. What did I ever do to be treated like this? Hell, most families treasure boys! Not this one.''

Harry drew himself up. ''Well, you've gotten what you wanted, Grandfather. You've gotten Megan in the role you've been grooming her for since you hired her. I, for one, don't see much of a place for me in this *family* company."

"Of course you have a place," Grandpa Joe snapped. "I haven't gotten around to your—"

"You never get around to me," Harry interrupted. "Just save it. Both of you just save it." He turned to Megan. "If you haven't figured it out, we're through." He turned back to his grandfather. "And as for you, you'll get what you want. My resignation. I'll fax written confirmation to you via Sally tomorrow."

And with that, Harry turned on his heel and left the room.

"Well," Joe said as he exhaled the long breath he'd been holding. "That certainly didn't go the way I planned."

Joe's words spurred an immobile Megan into action. Megan flew to her feet and began running out the door. Darci had said Harry was sensitive, and Harry had told Megan all about his aspirations and feelings toward his job and his family. She caught him at the elevator.

"It wasn't what it sounded like," she said. "I didn't know what he was going to do."

She'd never seen him so angry, not even in any of the times they'd fought. Still his words were spoken calmly and quietly, the deadly undertone enough of a poison to her ear.

"Megan, spare me. We had a great fling. I just

made the mistake of thinking you might be different from all the other women who have graced my bed.''

That hurt worse than a slap to the face. ''I am different,'' Megan said. She got into the elevator with him. ''Harry, I love you.''

He scoffed at that, giving a short snort of disbelief. ''Really. Words mean nothing, Megan. Did I ever tell you about the woman I dated when I was twenty-two? She told me she loved me. She said she wanted to be with me. Then I found out the truth. She was married. Married, Megan. She just wanted a younger man to toy with, to divert herself with something pleasurable while she waited for something better.''

''I wasn't toying with you,'' Megan said. She followed him into his hotel room.

Harry began to toss his clothes randomly into a suitcase. ''I don't know if I believe you. I don't know if I want to. All I do believe is that in the end you think of yourself first. You don't care about anyone except yourself and getting what you want. You don't care who you use to get there.''

He was leaving. She had to stop him. ''I did not use you. I love you.''

Her words fell short.

''Save it for someone else.'' Harry grabbed the suitcase and headed to the elevator.

As she ran after him, Megan had never felt such panic. How had the situation gotten so out of control? Worse, she wasn't sure what situation she was in, what battle she was fighting.

"Harry, we always said we'd talk. We'd communicate."

His face was an immobile mask, but knowing him as well as she did, she could see the hurt etched in the tight ridges around his mouth and the hard tilt of his jaw.

"We have nothing to say," he said.

The elevator door opened, Joe stepped out.

"Where do you think you're going?" he asked.

"To let you run your own show," Harry said. He stepped into the elevator and hit the button for the lobby. "After all, nothing I've ever done is good enough. You and your golden girl can handle tomorrow's media event. I'm taking a vacation effective immediately, and like I said, I'll fax my resignation tomorrow."

And before anyone could think to stop him, the doors closed and the elevator began to make its way downward. Megan took a step forward and stopped as Joe turned toward her.

"That boy always did have to pout," he said. "Don't worry. He'll see the light in a little bit. He always does. But right now business calls. I have a dinner meeting with the ambassador. There will just be one fewer of us. You are in, aren't you?"

There were no lights outside the elevators indicating what floors the cars were at. By the time she'd get to the lobby Harry would be long gone. She fought back the tears. She'd just have to trust Joe, although at this point that didn't sound like a good idea.

And God forgive her for not pursuing Harry, but she needed her job. She did need the promotion. The raise would go such a long way to helping out with her mother's medical bills.

"I'm in," Megan replied, a part of her dying inside as she spoke. "Just let me go change into a dress."

"I'll meet you in my suite," Joe said. "Ten minutes enough time?"

Oh God, what had she done?

"Plenty," Megan said, her heart not into the upcoming evening. "Just plenty."

"HARRY! WHAT ON EARTH are you doing here?" Darci took one look at the suitcase at his feet and was immediately concerned. "What's going on?"

Harry stepped into the foyer of his sister's apartment. "It's like you always said, 'If I didn't love Grandpa Joe.' In this case, if he wasn't family I'd throttle him."

"Oh no. Leave your suitcase and come out on the terrace with me. It's a gorgeous day and I was doing some reading. Can I get you something to drink?"

"Bourbon?"

Darci frowned as she contemplated his answer and Harry couldn't help but smile just a little. At least one thing in his world was certain—his sister's reactions. Of course the rest of his world had just gone to hell in a handbasket.

"I know," he said, "it's not even four. You don't need to lecture me about trying to drown my sorrows in alcohol and problems swimming. Do you have iced tea?''

"If you need it, I'll get you that bourbon."

What Harry needed was Megan, for the dream to have been real and not an illusion. "Iced tea is fine," he said.

"That I can do," Darci replied. She gestured to a table on the terrace. "I'll meet you there."

Harry stepped out onto the terrace. Overlooking Central Park, the view was fantastic. He put his hands on the brick railing and leaned over. He glanced to his right, down toward Times Square, which of course he couldn't see from here.

Darci had been right about the May day being wonderful. The temperature ranged in the mid seventies with no humidity, but even the great weather did little to warm Harry's heart.

Megan had sold him out, and his grandfather didn't care.

Not a good day by any measure.

Darci returned with a tall glass of iced tea. "You are going to tell me about it," she said.

"Yeah," Harry replied. He left his position by the wall and sat down at the table. He reached for the tall glass she was holding. "It's a doozy, let me tell you."

By the end of his tale Darci sat with a stunned look on her face. "And you're sure you didn't overhear him wrong?"

He'd been over it two dozen times by now. "I wish. No, I heard him correctly. His exact words are burned into my brain. 'I don't care about Harry. It's you right now that I'm concerned with. You're being promoted as soon as we return. How does vice president of development sound?' How can I misunderstand that? Tell me, Darci, because if there's any way I could have misunderstood, believe me, I'd love to think that in this case I was wrong.''

Darci tilted her head, her sympathy obvious. ''I'm sorry. I don't think so. Harry, I'm so sorry.''

''You and me both.'' Harry raked a hand through his blond hair. ''You know what really hurts, though, is that she said she loved me. Can you believe that? She told me she loved me. How can you love someone and walk all over them at the same time?''

Wisely Darci said nothing, just listened.

Suddenly Harry stood up and paced the terrace. ''I mean, what type of a fool does she think I am? I confided all sorts of things to her. She knew how important this promotion was, and she got it. I should have trusted my instincts. She's always been an opportunist.''

''Harry, I don't know what to say.''

''I know.'' Harry tossed his head to the side as if banishing horrible thoughts. ''Don't worry about it. There's nothing to say. I'm just grateful that you're here.''

''Where else would I be?'' Darci was almost in tears. She stood. ''You are my brother and despite our differences sometimes, I love you.''

Harry allowed himself to be dragged into his sister's arms for a much-needed hug.

''You know, Darci, that's at least one positive out

of all this. At least I never told her how I felt. At least I still have that sliver of my pride. Although I guess after all the women I've probably hurt without meaning to, it was bound to be my turn. What goes around comes around, doesn't it?''

He detached himself and reached for his iced tea. The ice cubes rattled in the empty glass. He looked at it in surprise. He couldn't remember finishing his drink.

Darci stepped back. "So what will you do now?''

Harry gave a short bitter laugh. ''I'm not sure. Live off my trust fund like Shane?''

Darci gave a slight shudder. ''No. That is not an option. You need to work. Cameron had to go into the office for a few hours today. He has a business deal in the works over in Asia, and with the date change, coordinating when everyone is awake versus asleep is next to impossible. He'll be home soon, and then we'll see what we can do.''

She placed her hand on her brother's arm. ''I know you thought I was only joking before, but O'Brien Publications will find you a home. You'd be a great addition, Harry. You are a good businessman.''

''Thanks.''

''Besides, I'd love having my brother in New York. There are lots of eligible women here, you know. I know a few book editors that you would really like. They edit romance novels of all things. Romance comprises over fifty percent of the market, you know.''

Although his heart wasn't in it, Harry gave Darci

his trademark lady-killer grin. "Maybe in a few months."

"Not a problem," Darci said. "When you're ready. Until then, let's get you set up in a guest bedroom. I'm assuming you're not headed home anytime soon?"

"I don't want to."

"Then don't."

"But I don't want to impose on you and Cameron either. It's not like I can't afford a hotel."

"Hotels are impersonal and you're not an imposition. You're my brother and I have four empty guest rooms. You can hide out here and conduct your business from either Cameron's or my offices. They're just down this hallway here."

Within minutes, Darci had established Harry into a guest bedroom. Her poor brother was absolutely emotionally drained, and she didn't blame him for wanting to simply lie down for a while.

Darci was waiting for her husband when he came home. Quickly she filled him in on the situation.

"The old meddling sot really did it this time," Cameron agreed. "Sure I can make a place for Harry. I'd be happy to if that's what he really wants."

Darci nodded thoughtfully. "It is, but I have an idea. Hold off on his start date for at least a week or so."

Cameron looked surprised. "Why? I could start him as early as Wednesday. With the buyout of Zenon, we're all overworked."

"No, let's wait. I'm hoping that maybe once tempers cool down in Saint Louis, Grandpa Joe will realize he's made a mistake. Of course, I doubt that he'll do anything about it, stubborn fool that he is. Don't get me wrong, you know I love my grandfather, but he did a bang-up job this time. Anyway, it's Megan I'm concerned about. Harry said she told him that she loved him. If she truly loves him, we need to give her some time to come to her senses and act. After all, you and I both know how pride can get in the way."

Cameron drew Darci into his arms. "Yes, I do. Your grandfather and my sister gave us a chance to work through it. We never would have spoken to each other again had they not interfered."

"Exactly. Now it's our turn to give Harry that same time. Let's not entrench him too fast into a decision he may regret later."

"No problem," Cameron said. He dropped a kiss on her lips and she eagerly responded. "How about a late nap?"

Darci laughed. "As if we ever sleep."

Chapter Twelve

Harry Sanders Personal Fax
212-555-6780
To: Joe Jacobsen
314-555-8900
Re: Resignation

As per our conversation today, I will be resigning effective June 10. Until that time, I will utilize the last of my vacation. I have called my father and mother and told them of my decision.
H.S.

Jacobsen Enterprises Internal Memo
From: Andrew Sanders, president
To: Joe Jacobsen, CEO
Re: Harry

Did I not warn you not to meddle? Let me tell you, your daughter Lily is not happy about this turn of

events. I expect you will be hearing from her soon if you haven't already.
A.S.

Jacobsen Enterprises Internal Memo
From: Joe Jacobsen, CEO
To: Andrew Sanders, president
Re: Harry

I've already heard from Lily and from my darling wife, Henrietta. Don't you start in on me as well. Despite this factor, Megan MacGregor has been promoted to vice president of development. I expect you to meet with her Thursday at one for a lunch meeting regarding her new position.
J.J.

"CONGRATULATIONS," Cheryl said as Megan stepped out of the elevator Thursday morning. "It's official. You're moving to the 24th floor tomorrow. I've got the moving paperwork right here. And don't forget, you've got lunch at one today with Mr. Sanders."

"Thanks," Megan said. "Don't forget, you're going upstairs with me." As part of her new position, Megan had been assigned her own secretary. She'd picked Cheryl to fill the role.

After Cheryl handed Megan her mail, Megan walked to her small cubicle. It was strange to think she was leaving it. To make it more real, she'd boxed up most of her things yesterday afternoon during a brief lull.

Lunch with Mr. Sanders at one. The president of

Jacobsen Enterprises was meeting her, Megan MacGregor, for lunch.

And after all, why not? She was now a vice president.

Her bubble burst. But Andrew Sanders was Harry's father. And she had the job Harry had wanted.

Megan sighed as the guilt consumed her again. The office grapevine had been buzzing ever since Monday afternoon when the contents of Harry's fax had become widely known. He'd resigned. He'd gone through with his threats to leave Jacobsen.

Grandpa Joe had sent out an e-mail to all employees announcing Megan's appointment the same day.

Since then, Megan had endured wary congratulations as people wondered why she'd been promoted over the grandson. Everyone would look at her curiously, wondering exactly what had happened in New York.

While no one knew the true nature of the personal matters between Harry and Megan, the fact that he'd been passed over for a vice presidency—again—had made the gossips stand longer than usual at the watercoolers and coffeepots.

Megan still didn't understand it herself, and so far she'd tried to avoid thinking about it or letting the guilt eat her alive.

Her mother and Bill had been thrilled for her. She'd achieved all she'd set out to do. But in the process she'd lost the man she loved, that half of herself she'd never missed before.

So lunch with Harry's father at one. She checked

her e-mail as she contemplated the meeting. What would she say to Andrew Sanders if he asked about his son?

Would she tell him that every time she thought about Harry she cried because it hurt so bad? That she didn't know anything about what Harry was doing or even if he was okay?

Several times she'd called Harry both at his condo in Clayton and on his cell phone. His cell phone was off—each time she'd immediately gotten the recorded greeting announcing he wasn't available. She'd left two messages pleading for him to call. She'd debated telling him she loved him, and broke down and told him anyway. He'd never called back.

Even Megan's mother, sensing her daughter's growing distraught state, hadn't known what to say, what advice to give once Megan told her the whole story yesterday.

So in the end Megan had done what she always did in a crisis—make lemonade from lemons. She buried herself in her work. It was 12:50 before she knew it.

"You are ready to go upstairs, aren't you?"

Megan jumped as Cheryl stepped into the cubicle. Megan glanced at her watch. She had just enough time to make it by the powder room and freshen up. "Thanks for reminding me. I got so busy with this Portland, Oregon, proposal that I lost track of time."

Megan took a moment to stretch out the kinks in her neck. How she longed for the time when Harry had given her that relaxing backrub and then tucked her into bed.

She grimaced. She couldn't dwell on the past. She had to go forward, even if forward without Harry wasn't necessarily the direction she wanted or ever envisioned herself going. Hadn't she warned herself to guard her heart? In the end, she hadn't listened. She'd fallen in love.

She stood. Great. Even though it was one of her new suits, from the store Harry had recommended— what? only a few weeks ago?—the suit was a plethora of wrinkles.

Oh well. The way Megan's life was, what were a few more wrinkles? The only bright spot was that her mother's new medications and monitoring had begun on Tuesday and so far she was doing well and improving. She'd even set a wedding date with Bill during Megan's time in New York.

Andrew Sanders's secretary announced Megan's arrival promptly at one.

"Ah, Megan," Andrew said as she entered the office. "It's good to see you." He stood, buttoned his suit jacket and came around from behind the desk to shake her hand. His grip was firm, like Harry's had been.

Now, standing in front of Harry's father, Megan could see where the younger Sanders got his good looks. Harry would age like this, she realized. The golden-boy locks would fade to a gray that was more white than silver. The lines around his eyes would crease more but the skin would still hold tight. His lips would still be full.

Harry stood as tall as his father, and Andrew gestured toward the door. "Mike Shannon's sound good? I took Darci there when she was promoted and no matter what Joe says, you can't eat at a Jacobsen establishment all the time."

"Fine," Megan replied. She'd never been in the broadcaster's signature restaurant. Within minutes they were seated at a private table.

Lunch turned out to be easier than Megan had expected. She and Andrew talked shop for most of the meal. He outlined her position and the responsibilities that came with it.

Megan was just starting to think she'd escaped any mention of Harry, when Andrew said, "Now that you're an executive, there's something you need to know. No matter how much he may think differently, Grandpa Joe shouldn't be such a meddler."

Megan set her fork down next to the Cobb salad she was almost finished eating. "Sir?"

"Andrew, call me Andrew. I'm sure you know what I'm talking about. Grandpa Joe and his matchmaking. Hell, I have to admit that I'm guilty too. When Grandpa Joe said double or nothing with Harry I didn't refuse. As if one can refuse Joe Jacobsen anything. But this time he went too far. He's run off my son and believe me, my wife is not happy about that."

"Harry's run off?"

"He's still in New York," Andrew said. "He's

living with Darci and her husband until he can find a place of his own. Seems he's going to work for O'Brien Publications as a vice president of something or other. From what Darci tells me, Harry starts in two weeks.''

The news was like a blow to Megan's stomach. She suddenly felt sick. Harry hadn't come home. He wasn't planning on ever returning to Saint Louis to live. When he'd said they were through, he'd really meant it.

Part of her had so hoped otherwise.

''I'm so sorry. This is all my fault. I was promoted into the spot he wanted.''

Andrew gave a dismissive wave of his hand. ''Let's put the blame where it squarely belongs. Harry's grandfather. It's a long story, and perhaps I shouldn't tell you this, but Harry's never quite lived up to Grandpa Joe's expectations. Harry's the oldest grandson, you see, and Grandpa Joe saw in Harry everything that he himself wished he could have been at that age. Unlike Grandpa Joe, Harry wouldn't have to struggle and build an empire from scratch. Under Grandpa Joe's tutelage, Harry would be able to truly soar. It's a lot of pressure on a child, and I'll admit, I didn't stop it as I should have.''

Andrew paused to sip his iced tea. ''Needless to say, Harry didn't finish Grandpa Joe's crazy scheme to indoctrinate his grandson into the company. Darci made it further, and when she and Cameron had their big fallout, Grandpa Joe promoted her, partially to make it up to her and partially to soften the blow of love gone wrong. It ended up okay, but of course Darci's promotion was a blow to Harry. He's just as smart as she is.''

''He told me about this,'' Megan said.

''So you understand. The funny thing is, though, Grandpa Joe can't make it up to Harry. Harry's had it, and refuses to take his calls. He also quit.''

''I shouldn't have been promoted,'' Megan said.

''Your promotion isn't the issue. You definitely deserve it. I've read the file. The issue is that Harry deserved a promotion as well. Joe should have made two, not just one, but as he didn't consult me first I had no say in the matter. Anyhow, since Harry is gone, you'll have to assume many of his duties. I'm also shifting several of them over to Jill Benedict. What you'll be responsible for is mainly—''

''I'm sorry, but I can't do this.''

''What?'' Andrew looked confused.

''I can't do this job. Not when it's cost Harry so much. You see, Joe was right about one thing. He was right about me and Harry. I love your son, Mr. Sanders, and if I take this position I'm just as bad as Harry says I am. I will have stepped on him, used him on my way to the top. If he's my future, then I need to show him that. It's not right that I take a job that rightfully belongs to him.''

Andrew Sanders leaned back in his chair. ''We've already gotten your nameplate on the door. Are you telling me you're quitting?''

Monetary figures ran rapidly through Megan's head. She was young and healthy. She could start over somewhere else. Her 401K plan could be busted to pay the rest of the outstanding medical bills. She could use COBRA, the government law that would let her continue her mother's health insurance for eighteen months. Her mother had finally agreed to set a date with Bill. She would be taken care of. Bill loved her. And Megan loved Harry. She looked at where Andrew sat waiting for an answer.

The words came out softly, and became louder as her resolve strengthened. "Yes. Yes, I think I'm resigning. I need to go to New York. I have unfinished business there."

Andrew cocked his head to one side. "This won't make Joe Jacobsen happy."

"No, but if I can convince Harry that we belong together then it will make me happy. Us happy. And I think Harry and I deserve that. True love only comes around once, and that's if you're lucky. I just hope he'll take me back. It's a risk, but I have to take it."

Andrew smiled encouragingly at her. "You make my son happy and you'll get my wife off my back. Tell you what. I'll hold your job for you for two weeks. I'm sure you have some vacation coming, right?"

"Only if you understand that I probably won't be back."

"You just let me know."

"I will." Megan glanced at her watch, suddenly unconcerned with whether the gesture was rude or not. She had to get to Harry. "Do you mind if I cut out early today? I've got a plane to catch."

"No." Andrew's eyes twinkled and Megan then noticed one difference between father and son. Harry's father had green eyes, eyes that were warm and encouraging. "I did tell you that Harry's staying with Darci, didn't I?"

"You did," Megan said. She stood. "Thank you."

With that she left the restaurant. Andrew watched her go. Yes, Grandpa Joe had been right. She was a class act through and through, and Andrew wouldn't be sorry at all to have her for a daughter-in-law.

He wished Megan luck as he paid the bill. He headed back to his office where he immediately had his secretary make a phone call. Ah, this next meeting was going to be particularly enjoyable.

Grandpa Joe arrived in Andrew's office less than ten minutes later. "What's this about an emergency?"

Andrew shrugged. "Megan took a leave of absence. A vacation. However, I must warn you, there's a very good possibility she might not be back."

"What!" Grandpa Joe's white beard bobbed. His blue eyes glared. "What did you do?"

"Nothing. I told her the details of her job, a job that she feels should rightfully belong to Harry. You were correct about that, she loves Harry. So much so that she's going to New York to convince him to take her back."

Grandpa Joe sat down in a leather armchair. "And you call me a meddler."

"No," Andrew said. "I'm undoing your meddling. As of this moment, all bets are off. If it works out, they'll get back together. And if you're lucky, the very least you'll have to do is beg both of them to come back to work for you. I can't wait to see that. I have a feeling that's going to cost you a great deal.''

Andrew smiled. ''Now, if you'll excuse me, I think Darci needs to know she's about to get a surprise visitor. There's enough that can go wrong, I think I'll remove just a few variables.''

''Hmmph,'' was all Grandpa Joe said.

''So you see why I have to go.'' Megan tossed clothes into a carry-on. She had to hurry or she'd be late for her flight. ''I love him, Mom.''

''You go, honey.'' Her mother smiled. ''Don't worry about me. Ever since I've told Bill I'd marry him, I can't get rid of him.''

As if that was a bad thing. It was fantastic to finally see her mother so happy. Megan had to give her one more reassurance. ''Money's not going to be an issue, Mom. I have it. It may be tight for a while, but don't worry. You concentrate on Bill and getting well.''

''You're my pride and joy, Megan. I'll be fine. You've done more than I ever needed. It's time for you to be happy.'' Megan's mom put her hand out and covered her daughter's. ''Go. Go win back that man you love.''

And two hours later, Megan found herself crammed in the rear of coach class on a New York-bound flight. Last-minute travel sure was costly, and Megan had maxxed out her charge card to pay for the flight.

But it didn't matter. Making Harry understand, that was what mattered.

Please let him speak to me. Please let him not slam the door in my face. She wouldn't know how he'd react until she got there, and the plane ride seemed to take forever. She couldn't read, and the baby in the mother's lap next to her never did stop crying.

It was nearly nine before she arrived at Darci's apartment. She approached the doorman, whom she knew needed to buzz her up. "I'm here to see Harry Sanders. I'm Megan MacGregor. He's staying with Darci O'Brien."

"One moment." The doorman walked to his phone and dialed a number. Megan waited impatiently, a small carry-on bag at her feet. She glanced at herself in a reflective wall panel. She was a miserable sight.

Her brown hair needed combing. Her lipstick was long gone. Her clothes, well, as always, those were a wrinkled mess. "Mrs. O'Brien has cleared you. You may go up," the doorman said.

Relief filled her. One hurdle down. Then again, what if Harry wasn't there? She decided to cross that bridge when she came to it. She'd made it this far.

The elevator doors opened and Megan walked to Darci's front door. Before she could knock, Darci opened it.

"My father called ahead," Darci said. Gone was the friendly tone of the late-Saturday evening they'd all shared on the terrace not even a week ago. "If you hurt him again, you deal with me."

"I never meant to hurt him," Megan said. She stepped into the foyer. "Is he here?"

"He's here. I didn't tell him you were coming." Darci reached for Megan's bag. She set it on the floor. "Follow me."

Darci led Megan to a small dayroom. "Wait here." Megan sat on the brocade sofa.

Darci wove her way through the back hallway and up the back staircase. She knocked on the door to Harry's room. "Harry? Harry, you have a visitor."

Harry opened the door and Darci's heart broke. She'd never seen her brother look so terrible. Despite his brave front and upcoming job at O'Brien Publications, he was still hurting. Lines that had never been there etched his face. "You have company."

"Company? At nine at night? I don't know anyone in New York. Send whoever it is away."

"I can't. You need to see this person."

"It's Grandpa Joe, isn't it? He's the last person I want to see. No." Harry began to close the door.

Darci put her hand out and stopped Harry's motion. "You need to see her. It's Megan. Dad called and told me she was on her way. If the suitcase downstairs is any indication, she's come straight from the airport."

Indecision and myriad emotions crossed Harry's face. "It's over," Harry said. "Send her away, Darci. I can't take seeing her."

"I told Dad you were as stubborn as Grandpa Joe. I told him."

"I am not like Grandpa Joe."

"Well, then, go talk to her. Prove it. I put her in the salon." And with that Darci walked away.

Harry stared at the back of his sister's retreating figure. Megan was here. She'd obviously flown all the way from Saint Louis to see him.

He could at least listen to what she had to say.

Unless he wanted to be as pathetic and stubborn as his grandfather, he could be man enough to deal with her. She couldn't hurt him again. He had no heart left to break. He went to face her.

Chapter Thirteen

"Oh, I didn't realize you were here." Cameron stood in the doorway to the salon. He studied Megan for a moment. Her clothes were rumpled. "Come to see Harry, I suppose."

Megan twisted her hands in her lap. Being that she'd been checking her watch constantly, she knew she'd been waiting about ten minutes now. "Yes."

"I'm glad," Cameron said. He leaned against the doorjamb.

"You may not be," Megan replied. "If it all works out right, then I'm probably going to need a job."

Cameron rubbed his chin as if massaging an imaginary itch. He'd already heard the story from Darci. "Another Jacobsen Enterprises resignation descending on the streets of New York?"

"Yes. Harry was right. I came as soon as I realized that. Hopefully it's not too late."

Cameron tilted his head and leaned slightly out the doorway. "Speaking of, I think I hear him and Darci coming now. Good luck."

Megan smiled wistfully. "Thanks. I think I'll need it. I hurt him pretty bad."

Cameron tapped his fingers on the door frame. "Just remember to be honest and lower that pride. You've come this far. You can go all the way."

Megan steeled herself as Cameron stepped out of sight somewhere down the hallway. She could do this. And if she failed, well, at least she'd tried. She'd given it her all. She'd never wonder what if, what if she wouldn't have at least attempted. That old cliché fit here. It was better to have loved and lost than never to have loved at all.

"Megan." Darci was back in the room. Her tone held an undercurrent of warning.

"Darci," Megan said. "Is Harry coming?"

"He's right behind me." Darci spoke a little louder this time. "Aren't you, Harry?"

Harry stepped into the room and immediately Megan's heart constricted and cried out for him. He looked, in a word…terrible. "I am."

"Harry," Megan said. She rose to her feet but his rigid posture made her stop before she took a step forward. Instead of looking directly at her, Harry had instead focused his attention on an oil painting hanging in between two windows. Megan knew her task wasn't going to be easy. This was a man who was really hurting, and she'd been the one to cause his pain.

"Darci?" Cameron's voice. He'd curved his body back around the doorway. "Didn't we have a movie we wanted to watch upstairs?"

"Oh? Yes." Coming to her senses, Darci scurried toward her husband. "We'll just leave you and..." She never finished as she and Cameron rushed off.

As soon as they left, the room grew quiet. Megan stood there, completely at a loss for what to do next. She'd never been in a situation like this before, pleading for the love of her life to forgive her.

"They certainly are happy. The perfect couple," she said to break the silence.

"Yes, they are." Harry turned toward her, giving Megan the opportunity to really study him. Dark circles graced his eyes, blue eyes that were cold and dead. Had she killed his hope? Megan's hands covered her mouth as the full horror of what she'd done hit her.

"Harry, I'm so sorry."

His eyes never seemed to blink. "For what?"

She stood there in disbelief. "For, for—" She stopped. Was there really a point? She hadn't expected him to be so cold, so distant. Well, she had, but not to this extent. This extent was practically insurmountable.

The echo of her mother's voice sounded deep in Megan's subconscious. "Go win back the man you love." All her mother wanted was for Megan to be happy.

Could she be happy? Her mother had managed, overcoming insurmountable odds. Her mother suffered from such a debilitating disease, yet each day she still grasped the brass ring fully. Megan's mother remained the eternal optimist.

Lemonade from lemons. She could do this.

"I'm here because I owe you an apology for a lot of things," Megan said. "You were right about me. I was greedy and I was selfish. While my intention was noble, that of helping my mother, I should have never stepped on you in the process."

She paused, but after a moment's silence it was obvious that Harry wasn't going to say anything yet. "I knew how much the job meant to you. When your grandfather hit me with the offer, I was stunned. I couldn't get a word in edgewise. And then you walked in."

"And spoiled your party." Bitterness laced his words, and Megan took a step toward him. She stopped as he stepped away.

"Things got out of hand quickly," she agreed. "I—"

Harry suddenly threw his hands into the air, a gesture of frustration. "We've been over this, Megan. I was there. Don't say anything else. It's not helping. Why are you here anyway? Did my grandfather send you?"

"No." Raw, burning hurt filled Megan, but she knew she had to press forward. She couldn't quit. Let him believe her. Please. "I came on my own."

"Why? I'm not returning to Saint Louis."

"I know. Your father told me."

Harry began to pace the small room, somehow still managing to avoid coming near Megan. "My father told you? What, are you having lunch with him?"

Would honesty ever reward her? It certainly hadn't

yet. *Come on, Harry, make this easier.* "Yes, actually I did. Today. Mike Shannon's. He said Grandpa Joe shouldn't have meddled."

Harry raked a hand through his blond hair and gave a short bitter laugh. "Like that's anything new. Let me guess, he took you there to fill you in on the details of your new position as vice president of development. After all, he took Darci there."

"That's how lunch began, but—"

But Harry now wanted to talk. "And he gave you some sob story of how my mother misses her son and so you decided to score brownie points and see if you could get me to come back home. Just save it. It's not going to work. Did the company at least pay for your airfare? I'd hate to think that you wasted any of your precious medical-bill money."

"It's not like that at all. It's—"

Harry stopped pacing for a moment. "Lies. You can stop lying to me now. I'm not your mentor. I'm not your boss. I'm just some guy who wants nothing more to do with you."

"Harry, I—"

Did the Jacobsen men make a habit of cutting people off? "Don't. It's been great seeing you, Megan, well, no not really. I'm not even going to pretend to be polite. Go home and tell my parents I'm fine, and tell my grandfather that he screwed up. You're his golden girl. He's only unhappy that I'm gone because my mother's on his back."

"Harry, damn it, you listen to me!"

Harry froze, the expression on his face almost comical. In all of his time dealing with Megan, he'd never heard her utter a cussword. She must really have a lot riding on this. "Why? Tell me—why should I?"

"Because I love you!"

He hadn't expected that particular hammer. Well, he had, but not at this particular time. He thought she'd have saved it for the last argument, for the last emotional appeal.

Thus, for a moment her declaration immobilized him, giving him a chance to really take in her appearance. She didn't look like a woman who now had it all.

No, she looked like a woman who had suffered a bad airplane flight. Her clothes were a wrinkled mess, her makeup smudged where it wasn't gone, and her brown hair desperately needing a combing. She looked wild, almost primal, the model of perfection long gone.

And the expression on her face—poker was not the game she was playing. Anger lingered there, and fury. But with those he also saw sadness, caring, passion, desire and frustration all rolled into a sea of expressions that flitted across her face.

He'd pushed all of her hot buttons, and she wasn't hiding it. But at the same time, she wasn't right back at him. She hadn't lashed out at him the way she had when they'd fought the day she'd discovered he was to be her mentor.

Of course, lashing out at him wouldn't achieve her objective, getting him home.

But those words, that declaration of love, how he

wished it could be enough. That it could be true. But he couldn't risk it. Not ever again. She'd hurt him too badly.

"It's not enough," he told her, and with that he left the room.

DARCI, NOT REALLY into the movie showing on the television in her bedroom, heard Harry's bedroom door slam. "Not good," she told her husband. She jumped to her feet. "Stubborn fool. Do me a favor. Go check on Megan. Is your father still out of town?"

"Yes. He's visiting Kit for another week."

"Great. Go install Megan over there. I'm going to go beat some sense into my brother. And believe me, this time he had better listen."

"MEGAN?"

Hearing Cameron's voice break through the silence, Megan looked up. She could hardly see him through the tears that were streaming down her face. "I failed."

"It's going to be okay," Cameron said, "but for now let's get you someplace to stay."

"I didn't make any reservations."

Cameron's sympathy tripled for her. She really had just left everything and shown up in New York. "My father is out on Long Island staying with my sister for a few weeks. Since we can't get him to sell his apartment, I'm going to take you there. No one else will be there, although the housekeeper will come in each morning. Now mind you, it's a monstrosity, but I guarantee you a soft bed.''

What else could she do? Harry had turned her away. Despair continued to fill her. But Cameron waited for her answer, and she did need a place to lick her wounds.

"Thanks," Megan said.

"No problem," Cameron said. "Let's go."

BECAUSE HE WAS listening for it, Harry heard the sound of the front door slam. He wasn't surprised when Darci barged into his bedroom less than five minutes later.

"There, she's gone." Darci said.

"Good," Harry said.

He tossed aside the magazine he'd been attempting to read. He wouldn't admit the words had blurred on the pages.

"I'm glad she's gone. It couldn't have been soon enough. If she comes back, tell the doorman to send her away."

Darci stared at him in disbelief.

"What?" Harry asked. "She failed to get me to return to Saint Louis. She might try again."

"You are such a stubborn fool. Sometimes I wonder how we are related at all! She traveled all this way because she loves you and you just rejected her!"

Right. Harry kicked his feet up onto the ottoman in front of the overstuffed chair he was sitting in. He took a deep, calming and cleansing breath.

Despite his outward appearance, seeing Megan had shaken him. His body still wanted her. His heart still loved her. His mind still needed her.

Would he ever be able to free himself? Tonight, at least, he had started. He'd been able to send her away. It had taken all of his mettle, all of his resolve. When she'd said she loved him....

She'd always have a part of him. She'd always have a piece of his soul, a portion of his heart. He'd never be able to replace them.

He was just so confused. The emotions tumbling inside him—hurt, anger, bitterness, yet still want, need, passion and love—those emotions were new to him. Foreign. Megan had unlocked all of them.

But then, people that lost limbs learned to live without them. He could live without whatever part of him she'd taken. Okay, poor analogy. But he'd learn to live without her. No matter how hard it hurt. He'd go on. He, Harry Sanders, would survive.

He realized Darci still waited in the room. "You're still here?"

"Yes. I see that I'm going to have to beat some sense into you."

He shrugged his shoulders. "Don't bother. I'll be happy to move out and get my own place, but I'm not going back to Saint Louis. That's why she's here. She had lunch with our father and now she's trying to win brownie points and get me to return."

"Oh my God." Darci covered her mouth with her hand. She then made a fist and shook it at him. "You are so blind. That is so far from the truth."

"How?" Had he missed something somewhere? He mentally ran over the conversation. He had cut Megan off a few times, but no, he didn't think he'd missed anything. "If you're so all wise, why don't you tell me what I missed?"

"Our father, speaking of, called me earlier today to tell me that Megan was on her way."

Harry jumped in. "See, that proves it."

"No, duncehead, it doesn't. It proves the opposite. She resigned. Megan quit that all-paying, all-wonderful promotion. Dad said Grandpa Joe didn't take the news very well."

"She quit." Disbelief stunned Harry and he sat there frozen. A sick feeling began to overtake him.

"One last time, yes, she quit." Darci leaned over Harry. "She told Dad that she didn't feel right doing a job that should rightfully belong to you. She told him she loved you, and that she was going to New York."

Harry now knew how passengers of the *Titanic* felt. They hadn't believed. They'd been wrong. He'd been wrong.

His words came out barely above a whisper. "Why didn't anyone tell me?"

"Because we thought it wasn't our place. You needed to hear it straight from her. You two have a lot to work out, that is if it's not too late."

Darci's last words sent Harry into a frantic panic. Was it too late for him and Megan? He deserved his own fate if it was. How often had he misjudged her? How often had he let his preconceived notions get in

the way? When it came to Megan, he'd been a fool.
She was nothing like any woman he'd ever known.
How could he have judged her by a set of standards
that didn't apply?

And he had.

He'd taken all his own biases and filters and seen
Megan through them. Her only crime was loving him.
Instead of talking to her about the promotion, he'd let
his anger at Grandpa Joe consume her as well. He'd
lumped them together—both guilty parties.

He'd made the worst tactical error of all. He hadn't
realized the truth—that in the end neither one was
playing a game. They were playing reality, for a love
that now lay in metaphorical tatters around his feet.

"So are you just going to sit there?"

Harry glanced up at his sister. She released her grip
on his chair, straightened and stepped back.

"I have to go after her."

"In the very least," Darci said. "She's staying at
Cameron's dad's place. The other side of the park.
Not too far." Darci rattled off an address and security
code. "I'll call the doorman and have him get you a
cab."

Harry was already putting on his shoes. "Thanks."

Darci shrugged and gave Harry *that* look. "What
are sisters for?"

She reached out and placed a hand on his shoulder.

"Harry, I just want you to be as happy as I am. I
never thought my life would blend with Cameron's.
We always seemed at cross-purposes. There was
something there, but it never seemed enough. You

know, that something may be small, but it's more
than enough. Once you release it, claim it, it's like a
box that never empties. Let her in, Harry. It may be
hard, but I guarantee you won't regret it. Keep in
touch.''

"I'll let you know.''

"Deal," Darci said. She enfolded her brother in a
brief hug. "Go."

As Harry left the bedroom and headed down the
stairs, she took a deep breath and said a silent prayer.
"Let it work," she whispered.

AFTER CAMERON LEFT, Megan wandered around Mi-
chael O'Brien's huge two-story apartment. Peeking
into all the rooms was like looking at an issue of
Architectural Digest. Everything was so perfect, not
one speck of dust allowed to linger. What a far cry
from the newspapers piling up on tables at home.

She ran her hand over the baby grand piano, pressing middle C. The pure sound echoed throughout the
two-story-high great room that was filled with the latest designer furniture.

Not knowing what else to do she walked over to
the floor-to-ceiling windows. The three layers of curtains were drawn back revealing a fantastic view.
Down below her the lights of Central Park flickered
through the trees like pixies, and across the way she
could see distant steady lights of other apartments.
Harry was somewhere over there.

She gripped her linen pants, fisting the material as
an outlet for her frustration. This huge expanse, al-

most four thousand square feet, was too much. Too quiet. It almost magnified the depression now raging through her.

She could watch television. In another room she'd discovered a fifty-two-inch HDTV complete with DVD player inset into custom wood cabinetry. Her exploration had also found a library of what looked like hundreds of DVDs. She returned to that room and began to peruse the titles.

But even thinking about movies reminded her of watching them with Harry. And so Megan simply sat on the burgundy leather sofa and wept.

"I can't stay here," she said aloud, the sound of her voice echoing off the walls. "This is not me." No matter the cost, she had to go to a hotel. A hotel was anonymous, like her.

She went to grab her suitcase out of the guest bedroom, a room also larger than all of her Saint Louis flat's rooms put together. She hauled the carry-on bag downstairs and paused at the front door. How did the security system work again? At home she just turned a key.

Maybe it just automatically started when she exited. She hoped so. She picked up her suitcase and opened the door.

"Hello, Megan," Harry said.

MEGAN BACKED AWAY from the door and set her suitcase down. Her heart gave a wary leap. Harry looked as if he'd pretty much rushed right over. "What are you doing here?"

"Can we talk?" He programmed a security code and then turned to her.

"I thought you said we finished talking."

"I made a mistake," Harry said. Something in his tone told her how serious he was and a small flicker of hope flared inside her.

"It seems like I've been making quite a few of those lately," he said. He saw her suitcase. "Are you going somewhere?"

"A hotel. It's sweet of Cameron to offer me somewhere to stay, but this place is too big, too empty. I can't stay here."

He nodded. "You're definitely not the flamboyant type."

"I never have been."

"I know that now. I'm extremely guilty of misjudging you. Quite a lot when I think about it. For that I'm truly sorry."

His words sent a shiver through her. To control the goose bumps covering her arm, she rubbed them through the long-sleeve blouse she was wearing. Had she heard him right? He'd apologized?

"I don't know what to say," Megan said, for honestly, she didn't. Her forehead creased. "Harry, what do you want from me?"

He stepped forward, close to her. Part of her waited for his touch, but before he made contact though, he dropped his hands to his sides. "You're perfect the way you are. It's me. I've been so foolish. You quit your job."

"Yes." She leaned her head to one side and studied him. As if he couldn't resist, he reached forward and tucked a loose strand of hair behind her left ear.

"I love the way your hair feels," he said. "How could I have been so wrong about something that feels so right? That is so right?"

His fingers moved to trace the lines creasing her face. His touch was soft, soothing, and his touch vanquished her deep furrows. "You love me."

"Of course I do." Love began to fill her torn heart, mending it and sewing it shut. A tear ran down her face and Harry captured it on his finger. He placed it to his lips as if memorizing the texture of it.

"You gave up your job, your life, and came after me."

Tears of happiness began to freely fall, and Harry reached forward to lift her chin. His blue eyes, those blue eyes she loved so much, were filled with something she'd never truly seen there before. She'd seen hints of it, glimmers, perhaps, but now it was all there. She could see all the love he had for her.

"Harry, you are my life," Megan said. "You're my other half. You make me whole."

The back of his hand traced her cheek. "I believe you. I'm so sorry I didn't before. I know my disbelief hurt you, and that's unacceptable. How could I have done it? How could I have hurt you when I love you so much?"

Love for this man overflowed and Megan reached out to touch the side of his face. He captured her palm and brought it to his lips.

"We each made mistakes," Megan said. "Oh,

Harry, we always will. But if we love each other, it'll always be okay.''

''And I do love you,'' Harry said. ''I should have told you earlier. Pride. Stubbornness. They're my biggest flaws. I failed to communicate.''

''We'll work on that,'' Megan said. ''We have the rest of our lives.''

''We do,'' Harry said. ''But I'm going to do this right. I don't want a live-in lover, Megan. Playboys have live-in lovers. I don't want that. I want it all. Commitment. Permanence. For better or worse. I know this isn't a romantic way to ask—no wine, no ring, no soft music—but Megan, will you marry me?''

Joy filled Megan and she reached forward and cupped his face in her hands. She stared into his eyes, her gaze never wavering. This was important. ''You know what makes romance, Harry? Love. The happy ending. Not wine or rings. Words. I love you. I will be honored to be your wife. Now kiss me.''

That he could do. Harry drew her into his arms, the motion feeling like nothing he'd ever experienced. His nirvana was Megan, and she was back where she belonged. As was he.

He kissed her slowly, tenderly, showing her every bit of the love he had for her. She was his woman, his other half, his world. Life without her just wasn't worth living. Together they could do anything.

So later, while curled up in bed, he broached their future again.

"You quit your job. I wish I could have seen my grandfather's face when my dad told him."

"I think I'm glad I don't have that memory," Megan said.

Harry rolled Megan on top of him so that he could see her face. "You're crazy, you know. You gave up the best job of your life to chase after me."

She angled herself onto an elbow and drew her chin up. A playful, loving expression crossed her face. "You know, you're right. I am crazy. Crazy in love with you. I'd have been a fool to work anywhere without you. But, after all, the job I gave up is nothing like the one I'm getting."

"And what one's that?"

"The one of being your wife."

With that, Harry had kissed her once more, ending all conversation. They'd surfaced again only as daylight began to seep in around the edges of the curtains.

"Are you always going to keep me up all night?" Megan asked.

"Absolutely," Harry said.

Megan playfully punched his arm, her motion meant as a joke. "How will we ever work?"

Harry propped himself up on his elbow. He grinned. "Who needs to work? Megan, I'll keep you safe. You'll never have to worry about money again. I have plenty. We can do whatever we want, your mother can have whatever treatment she needs."

His expression sobered and he traced her lips with his forefinger. "But I know you. You want to work until we have kids. And speaking of your mom, you want to live close to her, don't you?''

Using her tongue, she moistened the lips he'd just finished touching. ''Am I that transparent?''

He leaned down and kissed the tip of her nose. ''No. It's just a lucky guess. Besides, this ornate lifestyle isn't for you. You're a Midwestern girl. So problem solved. We go back to Saint Louis.''

''But you have a job here.''

''You give up one, I'll give up one,'' he teased. ''Besides, if we really want, I think I can get us back into Jacobsen.''

''Really?'' She ran a finger over his inner arm. How she loved touching him.

''Let me see. I know the president's wife and the CEO's daughter pretty well. Right now my mom's not happy. I think she might exert a little influence for us.''

''I guess there is a vice presidency open, and your dad said that another should have been created. How about co-vice presidents of development. So shall we go as a team?''

''Absolutely. We are a team. A husband-and-wife team.'' Harry pulled her closer. ''I really like the sound of that. Of course, I think we'll need to have some outrageous salary demands just for the principle of the thing. After all, my grandfather does need to pay up for his meddling. Maybe it'll teach him a lesson, though somehow I doubt it.''

''I agree. But on that note, you do know that you're going to have to make peace with your grandfather.

He does love you. He's just, well, as much as you don't want to admit it, he's like you. Stubborn. Full of pride.''

Harry reached for Megan's hand and enfolded it into his own. "I know. Just promise me you'll stand beside me while I do it.''

"Of course I will. Where else would I be? You know I'll always be here for you.''

A moment went by, and then Harry suddenly started toying with her fingers, bringing them suddenly to his lips. "You know, I'm still not tired.''

His meaning clear, Megan laughed. "Harry.''

"We have nowhere to be today,'' he said. He freed her hand and began to touch her lips with his fingers. Then he slid his first two fingers teasingly down the side of her neck, the action sending tremors clear down to Megan's toes.

"Since the sun's just about up, let's start the day off right,'' Harry whispered. "We can always sleep in. You know, get up about three if at all?''

"Three?''

But Harry lowered his mouth to her neck and began to plant enticing kisses all over her smooth skin. His nibbling lips sent shivers of delirious desire shooting through her. Any protest she had washed away.

Megan's body heated under his tantalizing touch, already anticipating the lovemaking to come. She stroked his back, running her fingers over his taut muscles. She would never get enough. It was a power she wouldn't mind ceding, as he had already given her the same power over him.

She would always love and want this man.

She managed a few last words in between his kisses. "Are you sure you aren't a vampire? Up all night, sleep all day?"

"Whatever I am, I'm yours."

His declaration washed over her and Megan closed her eyes as she let the sensation of Harry Sanders overtake her once again. "You'll always be mine," she replied. "I love you. Always."

And Harry believed.

Epilogue

Jacobsen Enterprises Internal Memo
From: Joe Jacobsen, CEO
To: Andrew Sanders, president
Re: Harry Sanders, executive vice president

Okay, stop keeping after me about this. My wife and my daughter are bad enough, and Harry and Megan are about to be married—just six weeks now.

Here it is, that ownership you all demand: PERHAPS I SHOULD NOT HAVE MEDDLED. There, is that good enough? It's all you're getting. After all, I was the one to first get them together and it all worked out in the end, even though I did have to beg for both of them to come back.

I'm sure you were delighted that both of them bled me dry in their salary and benefits demands. Well, they are worth it. Together they are a great team.

I'm just happy Harry decided to return to Saint Louis. Much to all of our delight, we are slowly rebuilding our relationship.

Thankfully, Megan's a great help in that regard. Did I not tell you that she was his perfect match? I know these things. Oh, and FYI, I'm delighted to report that her mother's progress with her medical treatments looks extremely promising.
J.J.

Jacobsen Enterprises Internal Memo
From: Andrew Sanders, president
To: Joe Jacobsen, CEO
Re: Harry

Thank goodness you're out of grandchildren from your daughter. Thanks to you my life is a frenzy of wedding preparations. Hopefully in six weeks everything can get back to normal.

But I know you. I pity Blake's kids, for since you can't leave well enough alone that means they're next. Who are you going to start with? Claire, Nick, Olivia or Shane? You can tell me tomorrow. See you on the links at seven.
A.S.

GRANDPA JOE set aside Andrew's memo. His son-in-law did know him too well.

And yes, Grandpa Joe had made mistakes with Harry. But despite his age—after all, he was seventy—he was still man enough to learn from them. In this case you could teach an old dog new tricks. That's why his business empire had grown so well.

But that's the way his life had always been. And

from out of the burnt ashes of their previous fiasco had risen a new relationship with Harry, one that daily brought the two men closer together.

Yes, his life did manage to always somehow work out in the end. It always had. And he just wanted his grandchildren to find happiness the way he had, and their parents had. Was that too much to ask?

In this day and age his grandchildren were so busy that they didn't take time out for love. And after all, in the end, love was what it was all about.

Grandpa Joe reread part of Andrew's e-mail. Yes, his son-in-law had him pegged. Grandpa Joe wasn't done matchmaking. He'd tell Andrew tomorrow that the answer was Shane.

Grandpa Joe reached forward and pressed the Send button of the e-mail program. There. His latest plan was now in motion.

* * * * *

Look for Shane's story,
Michele Dunaway's next
Harlequin American Romance,
in 2004.

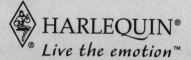

Forrester Square
LEGACIES · LIES · LOVE.

July 19, 1983...

The Kinards, the Richardses and the Webbers—Seattle's Kennedys. Their "compound"—elegant Forrester Square... until the fateful night that tore these families apart.

Twenty years later...

Their children were reunited. Repressed memories and family secrets were about to be revealed. And one person was out to make sure they never remembered...

Save $1.00 off
your purchase of any
Harlequin® Forrester Square title
on-sale August 2003 through July 2004

5 65373 00076 2   (8100) 0 11105

Visit us at www.eHarlequin.com
FSQ1OFFCOUPUS
© 2003 Harlequin Enterprises Ltd.

HARLEQUIN®
Live the emotion™

Forrester Square

LEGACIES · LIES · LOVE ·

July 19, 1983...

The Kinards, the Richardses and the Webbers—Seattle's
Kennedys. Their "compound"—elegant Forrester Square...
until the fateful night that tore these families apart.

Twenty years later...

Their children were reunited. Repressed memories and
family secrets were about to be revealed. And one person
was out to make sure they never remembered...

Save $1.00 off

your purchase of any
Harlequin® Forrester Square title
on-sale August 2003 through July 2004

5 2 6 0 5 2 3 1

HARLEQUIN®
Live the emotion™

Your opinion is important to us! Please take a few moments to share your thoughts with us about your experiences with Harlequin and Silhouette books. Your comments will be very useful in ensuring that we deliver books you love to read.
Please take a few minutes to complete the questionnaire, then send it to us at the address below.

Send your completed questionnaires to:
Harlequin/Silhouette Reader Survey, P.O. Box 9046, Buffalo, NY 14269-9046

1. As you may know, there are many different lines under the Harlequin and Silhouette brands. Each of the lines is listed below. Please check the box that most represents your reading habit for each line.

Line	Currently read this line	Do not read this line	Not sure if I read this line
Harlequin American Romance	❑	❑	❑
Harlequin Duets	❑	❑	❑
Harlequin Romance	❑	❑	❑
Harlequin Historicals	❑	❑	❑
Harlequin Superromance	❑	❑	❑
Harlequin Intrigue	❑	❑	❑
Harlequin Presents	❑	❑	❑
Harlequin Temptation	❑	❑	❑
Harlequin Blaze	❑	❑	❑
Silhouette Special Edition	❑	❑	❑
Silhouette Romance	❑	❑	❑
Silhouette Intimate Moments	❑	❑	❑
Silhouette Desire	❑	❑	❑

2. Which of the following best describes why you bought *this book?* One answer only, please.

the picture on the cover	❑	the title	❑
the author	❑	the line is one I read often	❑
part of a miniseries	❑	saw an ad in another book	❑
saw an ad in a magazine/newsletter	❑	a friend told me about it	❑
I borrowed/was given this book	❑	other: _____	❑

3. Where did you buy *this book?* One answer only, please.

at Barnes & Noble	❑	at a grocery store	❑
at Waldenbooks	❑	at a drugstore	❑
at Borders	❑	on eHarlequin.com Web site	❑
at another bookstore	❑	from another Web site	❑
at Wal-Mart	❑	Harlequin/Silhouette Reader	
at Target	❑	Service/through the mail	❑
at Kmart	❑	used books from anywhere	❑
at another department store or mass merchandiser	❑	I borrowed/was given this book	❑

4. On average, how many Harlequin and Silhouette books do you buy at one time?

I buy _____ books at one time ❑
I rarely buy a book ❑

MRQ403HAR-1A

5. How many times per month do you shop for any *Harlequin and/or Silhouette* books?
One answer only, please.

1 or more times a week	❏	a few times per year	❏
1 to 3 times per month	❏	less often than once a year	❏
1 to 2 times every 3 months	❏	never	❏

6. When you think of your ideal heroine, which *one* statement describes her the best?
One answer only, please.

She's a woman who is strong-willed	❏	She's a desirable woman	❏
She's a woman who is needed by others	❏	She's a powerful woman	❏
She's a woman who is taken care of	❏	She's a passionate woman	❏
She's an adventurous woman		She's a sensitive woman	❏

7. The following statements describe types or genres of books that you may be interested in reading. Pick *up to 2 types* of books that you are most interested in.

I like to read about truly romantic relationships	❏
I like to read stories that are sexy romances	❏
I like to read romantic comedies	❏
I like to read a romantic mystery/suspense	❏
I like to read about romantic adventures	❏
I like to read romance stories that involve family	❏
I like to read about a romance in times or places that I have never seen	❏
Other: _____	❏

The following questions help us to group your answers with those readers who are similar to you. Your answers will remain confidential.

8. Please record your year of birth below.

19 ____

9. What is your marital status?

single ❏   married ❏   common-law ❏   widowed ❏
divorced/separated ❏

10. Do you have children 18 years of age or younger currently living at home?

yes ❏   no ❏

11. Which of the following best describes your employment status?

employed full-time or part-time ❏   homemaker ❏   student ❏
retired ❏   unemployed ❏

12. Do you have access to the Internet from either home or work?

yes ❏   no ❏

13. Have you ever visited eHarlequin.com?

yes ❏   no ❏

14. What state do you live in?

_____

15. Are you a member of Harlequin/Silhouette Reader Service?

yes ❏   Account # _____   no ❏   MRQ403HAR-1B